LET ME FIND OUT 2

TERRANCE HOWARD

CHAPTER 1

"SECRECY IS DEADLY"
(FEDERAL ROAD)
HOUSTON, TEXAS

Redline quickly began searching through the thoughts that bombarded his mind. He laid there realizing certain things. Hollywood was far from stupid, and love and life were both bitches. Once you stuck your dick into them, you might as well enjoy, because a nut is bound to come. It always must end. He knew he was Hollywood's love and life...but the nut finally came...was this the end?

Having a ride and die chick does have its advantages. But when you're staring down the barrel of a gun with her tears falling in your face, it's clear that mistakes can be crucial. Secrecy can be deadly...love is the killer, and someone found out!

(THE GUN DISCHARGES!)

(BOOM! YEAH, SOMEONE FOUND OUT...)

The impact from the backhand Redline swung caused Hollywood's finger to involuntarily squeeze the trigger. Her vision was blurry from the tears she was raining down on Redline's face, which made her eyesight double. The bullet slammed through the pillow with such force causing lint to float throughout the air. Hollywood covered her face as Redline began slapping her as if she was a whore. She balled up drawing her knees against her chest tucking her face between her arms. Redline started kicking her body before snapping to his senses. This was his first time ever placing his hands on her. The way she was curled up on the floor crying and holding her bleeding mouth had him at a standstill.

Redline picked her up and carried her to the bathroom and gently sat her down in the bathtub. Hollywood kept her head down hiding her face as her tears were attempting to reach the drain. Redline stepped into the tub with her turning on the water. He soaked a towel underneath the warm flowing water then began wiping the blood from her face. Hollywoood tried pushing his hands away, but it was a waste of effort. He continued to clean the blood from her face. The more blood he wiped away the angrier he became with himself. He knew how she felt for her brother Pee Wee, and her actions didn't come as a surprise. The only thing that surprised him was the way he reacted to the situation.

"Baby I know you don't wanna talk to me right now. But I'm sorry," Redline said, raising her chin up. "I'm not gonna sit up here and try to make up an excuse. Plain and simple, I fucked up," he reached out again holding her head up. "The answer to your first question. I know Fast Blacc from the penitentiary, me and him did time together on Coffield. I met him out there in Killeen through my homeboy Tron."

Hollywood was sitting there listening.

"The answer to your second question. Me and Fast Blacc don't have a mutha fuckin' thing going on. We never had, and we never will," he explained, hoping she would forgive him for his rage of violence. "And the answer to your last question. I don't know if Fast Blacc killed Pee Wee or not. The only thing I know is what you told me," said Redline, turning the shower on.

He pulled her to her feet brushing the strands of hair away from her face. Redline gazed into her eyes slowly kissing away the blood from her lips. The water cascaded down their bodies washing blood and tears down the drain far away, but not far enough to be forgotten.

Hollywood felt what she did may have been stupid, but her mind was only focused on getting answers. She thought about what Redline told her. Did she jump to conclusions, or was the way she acted justified by the love she had for her brother?

"I'm sorry for pulling that gun out on you," Hollywood told him, hugging him tightly feeling bad about what she did.

Redline lathered up a towel bathing her from head to toe. He made a major mistake, hoping it didn't scar his relationship with her. He had to act quick in order to put this glitch behind him and Hollywood. After he saw the outcome firsthand and how it affected her, he vowed never to commit those actions again. He knew what Hollywood was capable of doing, and it was real dangerous allowing her time to think. Redline dried her off before carrying her into the bedroom. They both lay down together until she fell asleep. Redline stayed up thinking over his problems and many solutions. He quietly eased out of the bed and put on his clothes.

"They say the early bird gets the worm. So, I guess the early nigga gets the snake," He said to himself, gazing down at Hollywood as she was sleeping.

Checking his nickel-plated .45 automatic, he was satisfied with a full clip. When Redline had seen Fast Blacc in the mall his blood was boiling to the point of illogical thinking. The sound of Hollywood's voice brought him back to his common senses, making him remember the concrete hell hole he had just left. There was no time for rookie mistakes. Redline felt he had too much to lose. The faster the problem was solved the better.

(A FOOL ACTS OUT IN ANGER. BUT A SMART MAN TAKES HIS TIME TO PREPARE AND PLOT EACH SITUATION TO THE FULLEST.)

CHAPTER 2

"MORE THAN A ONE NIGHT STAND"
(CROWN PLAZA MOTEL)
HOUSTON, TEXAS

Lyric was still looking for another home. The only problem she had was finding a good location that she liked. Her and Amber have become sort of a couple, but neither of the two made anything official. Lyric's feelings for Amber were strong and indescribable. They've both been staying in a motel room since her home burned down.

Amber has been on vacation for a month. She didn't have a clue in her mind when or if she would ever return to work. Her and Lyric lay in bed together. Lyric was rubbing over Amber's body while giving her the scoop on what happened with Mona at the warehouse.

"Baby that feels so good!" Amber moaned out, while Lyric was kneading her body from head to toe. Lyric told her exactly how things occurred the day she killed Mona.

$$\$\$\$$$

"Now I got something hot for your ass bitch," Mona had said, as she reached the bottom of the stairs holding a pot of boiling hot water. "Since you like to see people get burned, let me see how you like this," Mona grunted, throwing the boiling hot water towards Lyric.

Lyric made it out of the restraints that bound her just in time.

Lyric was to light in the ass for Mona, so Mona took advantage of the opportunity. She slung Lyric's petite body against the side of the empty pool. Mona attacked her with a quickness. She kicked Lyric in the midsection so hard that Lyric hollered out in pain. Mona reached down and grabbed a handful of Lyric's hair with her left hand, and commenced to driving punches to her face. Lyric found enough strength and punched Mona in the stomach, knocking the wind out of her. Lyric tried to kick Mona in the face while she was down on her hands and knees gasping for air.

Mona was expecting the kick and grabbed Lyric's leg and flung her down. The good LORD was on Lyric's side. When she reached up for the edge of the pool to pull herself up, her hand landed on top of the gun Mona sat down by the pool side. Lyric turned around with only one thing on her mind, and that was putting Mona to sleep.

Lyric aimed the gun and squeezed off three quick shots which all pierced Mona's chest. Mona had a look of surprise on her face as she melted down to her knees. Lyric pointed the gun at Mona's face, closed her eyes, and pulled the trigger.

$$\$\$\$$$

Amber sat straight up gaping at Lyric, she couldn't believe what she heard. Amber's thoughts began racing. She knew this madness wasn't for her. She was used to chasing the dead presidents (MONEY) and being chased by a lunatic was something new to her. Her love for Lyric had her thinking totally out of character. Her mind was saying, "GO"- but her body was saying, "STAY".

"Lyric, I don't know what to say baby. I'm just glad you're alive," Amber said, rubbing Lyric gently across her face. "I never been the type of bitch to tuck my tail and run when a friend needs help," she told her, kissing Lyric on the lips with passion, thinking about what she was getting herself into.

Deep in her mind Amber felt she had to help finish what they started. Lyric knew this ordeal was out of her league. However, she had a maniac on her trail and her life was on the line, so she had to get her heart right.

"I'm sorry for getting you caught up in this madness. I should've kept my mouth shut, and none of this shit would've happened," Lyric said, with tears crawling down her cheeks.

Amber was feeling her pain even more than she was. If Lyric wouldn't have given her the information on Fast Blacc, she wouldn't have been involved. Lyric could have kept her mouth closed and not said anything, but she chose not to. Amber wiped the tears off Lyric's face.

"This ain't the time to be acting all soft and shit, it's too late for that. We have to prepare ourselves for the worse, and dictate our moves for the best," Amber told her, knowing it was all about do or die until Fast Blacc was dead or in jail.

Amber thought about Redline being out of prison, and how he was supposed to be taking care of Fast Blacc. Her and Lyric haven't heard from Hollywood since Redline had been home. Amber felt she knew the reason why? How could she blame Hollywood for being happy and enjoying her man who has been away for eight years? Amber envied Hollywood because she was receiving that fat dick Redline was packing. Her pussy became moist thinking about how Redline used to hammer her asshole in with hard fast strokes.

Amber pulled Lyric down on top of her, guiding Lyric's hand between her legs. Lyric let her fingers do the talking, kissing Amber's erect nipples. Amber took control and threw Lyric down on her back, positioning her sweet pussy on her face.

Lyric wasted no time licking the juices oozing from Amber's freshly shaved pussy. Amber placed both of her hands on the headboard riding Lyric's face as if it was a mechanical bull. She leaned her head back enjoying Lyric's tongue penetrating her hot, red snapper. Lyric navigated her tongue with precise skill and pressure, spreading Amber's delicate velvet lips. Amber tightened her thighs locking them around Lyric's face like they were vise grips, shaking with ecstasy. Amber twisted her body around in a sixty-nine-position returning the favor with gratitude. Lyric came with ease grinding on Amber's tongue with slow, hard rocking motions. Amber came again from Lyric's fingers moon walking inside of her pussy.

They cuddled up afterwards, each lost deep in their own world.

Amber had her thoughts on the drama she got herself into. It was too late to turn back. Plus, the love she was feeling for Lyric, didn't make her decisions any easier. Amber fell asleep thinking about Hollywood and the day Fast Blacc was about to rape her.

Lyric fell asleep with only one thing on her mind, and it wasn't the safety for her own life. Visions of Amber were floating throughout her dreams like she was in heaven gazing at one of GOD's angels. Lyric wore a smile on her face dreaming of happiness.

(DEATH AND DESTRUCTION CAN NEVER BE SATISFIED, AND NEITHER CAN THE EYES OF MEN.)

CHAPTER 3

"INDECISIVE THOUGHT"
(FEDERAL ROAD)
HOUSTON, TEXAS

Since the night of their altercation Hollywood hasn't left home because of her bruises. It's been a week since the incident. She was healing fast and her marks were barely noticeable. Hollywood tried her best not to hold any grudges against Redline, but certain things can never be forgotten.

Her mind flashed back to the night she pulled the gun on Redline while he was sleeping. She had the gun pointed in his face as she questioned him about Fast Blacc and her brother's murder. Hollywood saw something she recognized as fear from within. It was like Redline was hiding something from her, but she couldn't put her finger on it. Her mind was consumed with so many emotions that she couldn't think straight at the time like she normally would have. As she held the gun against his nose, she saw something she had never seen in him before.

Hollywood thought back to the day at the mall when they crossed paths with Fast Blacc. Redline stood there gazing at Fast Blacc like he was scared to be the man she knew he was, or who she thought he was. She saw indecisiveness written all over his face. If only she was carrying a weapon. Everything would have been over and done with, broadcasting live on the Channel 2 news at the First Colony Mall. The hairs on the back of her neck stood up, thinking about the man she would die for if things ever came to that point.

Hollywood wondered if prison had turned him into a pussy. A lot of scenarios were running through her mind rapidly. Hollywood came to the decision that she was going to play dumb and watch as things slowly unfold. She refused to believe the man she loves had turned into what the streets would label as a bitch ass nigga. She knew Fast Blacc wasn't the type of nigga you could just run over. She wondered why Redline was acting cowardly. It was hard for her to accept that her man was so leery of one person, after everything she told him that had happened. The word cautious bounced around in her head. Just to think about her man being scared, was really scaring her.

Hollywood wasn't your average female, she believed in half of what she heard and only what she saw. And from what her eyes were seeing, she knew it was time to investigate for herself. Redline had kept her Charles Bronson .38 Special. So, now she had to find herself another gun, which was very easy in HTown (*Houston*). Hollywood said a silent prayer for her brother Pee Wee. A lonely tear began falling down her cheek.

(A LOT OF PEOPLE NEED A CLIQUE WITH A LEADER, BUT EVERYTHING IS UP TO GOD IF WE GET OUR ENEMIES OR NOT).

CHAPTER 4

"COINCIDENCE"
(DENNY'S RESTAURANT)
KILLEEN, TEXAS

Tron has been calling Fast Blacc for a week, trying to find out if he knew anything about the shootings at the warehouse. Tron knew something wasn't right, and he felt Fast Blacc had something to do with it, or at least knew who did. Fast Blacc finally answered his phone.

"Yeah, what's jumpin' pimp? Volume down," Fast Blacc said, turning down the music on his voice activated JVC sound system.

"Damn nigga! I been trying to call your ass for a week. Where you been?" Tron asked, looking for an answer but not expecting the truth.

"Man, I been at the boat down there in Louisiana, with this lil' freak Tiffany. We been gambling, fuckin, and suckin you feel me?" Fast Blacc responded, trying to sense if Tron was buying his lie.

"Bug got killed at the warehouse last week, and me and Lil' Branon been trying to call you to see if you knew about it," Tron said, firing up a freshly rolled cigarillo filled with orange kush.

"Look out, meet me at Denny's off of HWY 190 so we can rap face to face," Fast Blacc told him, ending the call then ordering the volume to be raised back up on his stereo system.

Fast Blacc was jamming to some old school Ice T screwed and chopped. "ORAGANIZE CRIMER, BIG TROUBLE FINDER. IN AND OUT OF INSTITUTIONS EVER SINCE I WAS A MINOR.

NOW I'M IN THE MIX, DEEP IN THE FIX. CRIME SMART SEARCHING HARD FOR SOME NEW STREET TRICKS."

Tron's mind was grasping at different thoughts of him and his cousin Bug throughout the years of growing up. He couldn't understand how Bug was killed without a clue from anyone. After all the drama and crimes they've committed together, this was hard for Tron to swallow. Lil' Branon didn't say too much, but Tron knew he felt the same way about the situation. How could someone get murdered on their own turf without anyone knowing?

The police said there was a female found dead along with Bug also. She was shot at close range by the same handgun. Tron thought for someone to get the upper hand on Bug they had to know each other. Bug wasn't the type of person to just let anybody inside of his immediate circle. And if he did, he wasn't dumb enough to turn his back to them. Tron pulled on the cigarillo deeply inhaling the orange kush.

The early morning high was the best, so he was feeling proper exiting off HWY 190. Tron turned into the Denny's parking lot. His eyes immediately began searching for a parking spot. Soon as he located a parking place, the cigarillo fell on his lap as he was maneuvering the steering wheel. The velour sweat suit he was wearing began sizzling upon contact. He was so busy trying to knock the burning cigarillo from his lap, he almost crashed into a car parked next to him.

Tron slammed on his brakes coming to a sudden halt. He looked up into the face of a person he hadn't seen in many years. Tron recognized the person instantly, standing there in army fatigue wear, with a diamond encrusted dog tag hanging around his neck. Big four carat diamond earrings were hanging from each of his earlobes as if they weighed a pound. A diamond, individual set four-carat necklace dangled from around his neck also, displaying the colors of the rainbow. His hair was filled with so many waves, Surfside beach in Galveston had to be closed. Tron watched him standing there shaking his head with the likeness of the rapper Nelly.

Tron reversed his vehicle then eased into the parking spot correctly. He reached down picking up the reason for his near accident. Tron flicked the cigarillo away stepping out of his car brushing off the ashes from his burned sweatpants.

"Shit, I don't have to ask you if that's some good or not, the way you almost ran into my ride."

"My bad my nigga, but when that fire gets to burning you lose all focus," Tron said laughing, shaking his homeboy's hand while giving him a manly hug.

"I ain't trippin' my nigga. I almost ran into the back of a Metro bus when that same shit happened to me. But I had on them nylon Nike sweatpants, and you know how fast them hoes melt," he said, as they both began laughing.

While they were talking Tron saw Fast Blacc's car pulling into the parking lot. Fast Blacc peered at them with a sense of betrayal, reaching for the Glock .380 sitting in his lap. Before Tron even had a chance to open his mouth, Fast Blacc lowered his window and let his .380 vomit. Tron and his homeboy dove behind a car as bullets were touching everything in the parking lot. Thick white smoke began rising in the air throughout the parking lot. The smell of burning rubber became stronger as Fast Blacc made his escape.

Fast Blacc was sweating like an escape convict, and his heart was pumping like the pistons in the car he was driving.

"How in the hell did he find Tron? What the fuck were they talkin' about? I wonder who else was with them?" Fast Blacc thought to himself, nervously. Question after question ran through his brain while the answers remained a mystery.

His eyes darted back and forth looking in all his mirrors as if he was watching a ping pong match. Fast Blacc wondered if Redline was trying to eliminate Tron and the rest of his associates? Just the sight of Redline had Fast Blacc on the edge because he knew what Redline was capable of doing. If a nigga could call shots from behind prison walls, Fast Blacc could only imagine the things he could do now that he was free. Fast Blacc was mad at himself for not contemplating and reacting the way he did. Now he had to worry about Redline and Tron.

"No mistakes no mercy nigga!" He said to himself, turning the defrost on high blazing up a sherm.

Now things have changed from having the ups and being the hunter, to watching his back and being hunted. Fast Blacc didn't regret his decision. He was at the point where he had to shoot first and ask questions later. He thought about how he should've killed Lyric, Miss Stacks, and Hollywood when he had the chance. Now he had them, plus Tron and Redline to worry about. The odds were stacking up against him, and his downfall was himself. One thing he knew for sure, he wasn't going to get caught with his pants down taking a shit again.

He dialed Tiffany's number in search of a place to chill and calm his nerves.

"Hello!" She answered.

"What's up sexy?" Fast Blacc asked.

"Not too much this way. What's up?"

"I'm finna swing your way if you're not busy," Fast Blacc said, enjoying the effects of the sherm kicking in.

"It's cool, I don't have nothing planned for today anyway."

"Alright then I'll holla at you," Fast Blacc told her, ending the call.

He knew he had to come correct with his A game, no ifs, ands, or buts about it. He just needed time to plan and sort his way through this collateral.

(NEVER TURN YOUR BACK ON A FRIEND. AND WHEN YOU'RE IN TROUBLE, NEVER RUN TO YOUR FAMILY...WHY BRING TROUBLE THEIR WAY?)

CHAPTER 5

"MIND GAMES"
(FEDERAL ROAD)
HOUSTON, TEXAS

After the shooting took place Redline drove back to H-Town. He had a lot of plotting and scheming to do, and he also had to keep his eyes on Hollywood. As quickly as everything happened, he came to realize Fast Blacc was a bigger threat than he first conceived. Any imbecile that would jeopardize his own homeboy's life just to kill the enemy, must be deranged.

"With friends like that who needs enemies?" Redline thought to himself grimly.

His gaze drifted to Hollywood's Lexus SUV in the driveway next to his CTS with the factory shoes (*rims*) and limo-tinted windows.

"Man, I hope she ain't doing no trippin' today," He thought to himself, narrowing his eyes towards the front door.

Redline walked into the house and the aroma of fried fish entered his nostrils, making his mouth water like a hungry mutt. Hollywood had all the qualities in a woman any man could wish for. Redline knew he was overlooking her real love by focusing on what she knew about Fast Blacc. It was hard to evaluate Hollywood because her evasive nature kept everything undercover. And by knowing her so well, Redline was bothered by the thoughts concealed in her brain. He couldn't determine if she was telling him everything she knew, or if she was holding out.

The last time Redline faced off with Fast Blacc, Hollywood acted out from anger and frustration. Fast Blacc didn't pose a threat at that particular time. So, when he opened fire on him and Tron, that came as a total surprise. Redline wanted to return the gesture, he had .45 ways to make Fast Blacc pay attention. However, there was too much chaos and way too many witnesses screaming, gaping, and diving for protection.

Redline chose to be the smarter man, because in prison he practiced patience, planning, and preparation. He knew once he mastered the three P's, he would have a step above the rest. Redline was racing against his own destiny, because the streets were just like time...they never stop for anyone. He had to think fast. He had to be smart. Redline had to be careful not to slip on his own banana peel. The only downfall he was up against was himself...or was it Hollywood? That thought stayed on his brain as he prepared himself for his prey.

(THE FIRST PERSON WHO SPEAKS THEIR MIND, IT WILL ALWAYS SOUNDS GOOD...UNTIL SOMEONE STARTS ASKING QUESTIONS.)

CHAPTER 6

"DOWN TO RIDE"
(TOP'S BUTT NAKED CLUB)
KILLEEN, TEXAS

Tron drove to Lil' Branon's strip club to enlighten him about Fast Blacc. He had a feeling Lil' Branon wasn't going to be surprised about the ordeal. Tron knew Fast Blacc had something to do with Bug getting killed, and the bullets that talked shit earlier confirmed it all. Tron made eye contact with Fast Blacc well before he lit the parking lot up like the fourth of July. He thought about Redline, as a slow smile stole across his face. He didn't think he would see Redline so soon.

Tron used to score his books from Redline before he got locked up, things were clicking like clockwork back then. Lil' Reggie used to call Tron twice a month for a total of six books. Tron thought Lil' Reggie's record label slowed him down, and that was why he only called once a month. Then, the more Tron thought about it, Redline was dropping out way more than Himee was. When you're used to making a certain amount of money it becomes a routine, and when things start to change, so does that person.

Tron pulled into the club's parking lot. Even though it was two o'clock in the afternoon, there were a lot of cars already in the parking lot. He saw Lil' Branon leaning inside of Ke Ke's car kissing her through the lowered window. Ke Ke reversed her car blowing her horn at Tron. She turned her music up raising the peace sign out of her sunroof before driving away. Tron smiled because he was usually doing the exact same thing to her. He shook his head hopping out of his car.

"Damn my nigga, Ke Ke getting a little fly ain't she?" Tron said, closing his car door.

"Man, you know my babys' a G," Lil' Branon told him, reaching out shaking his hand. Lil' Branon glowered at Tron's car silently inventorying the damage.

"That's why I'm over here so I can tell you what went down," Tron said, adjusting the gun underneath his shirt walking into the club. He followed Lil' Branon into his office.

"What happened man?" Lil' Branon asked, as soon as the door closed.

"You probably won't believe me when I tell you," Tron told him, walking over to the mini bar to fix himself a drink.

"It don't matter if I believe you or not. What's up? What the fuck do you wanna do?" Lil' Branon responded, folding back his desktop revealing a hidden arsenal.

Tron's dark pupils gleamed at Lil' Branon digesting what he said. By the time Tron finished explaining the episode, Lil' Branon was more than eager for revenge. He already had a bad vibe about Fast Blacc, and what Tron told him only set things into motion. Tron didn't know why Fast Blacc betrayed the loyalty amongst them, and it wasn't going to take him long to find out. He cast a glance at Lil' Branon fondling over the selection of weapons.

"Don't worry about it Bug. We gonna ride on your enemies," Tron mumbled to himself, narrowing his eyes reaching for a 9mm Uzi screwing the silencer into place.

(EVERY SMART MAN ACTS OUT WITH KNOWLEDGE, AND A FOOL EXPOSES HIS HAND. REVENGE IS A DISH BEST SERVED COLD, SO ALWAYS THINK OF A COLD-HEARTED WAY TO FREEZE A MUTHA FUCKA.)

CHAPTER 7

"DECISIONS"
(CROWN PLAZA MOTEL)
HOUSTON, TEXAS

Amber was still indecisive on whether to stay in H-Town with Lyric or return to work. She had a little money saved away for rainy days, but Amber was so used to being on her hustle. And not being able to make some easy money was eating at her conscience like a drug addict. Lyric was preparing herself, getting ready for work. Neither one of them had heard anything about Fast Blacc, which was a good thing.

"Lyric, I think I might go back to work this week," Amber said, ignoring Lyric wincing at her words.

"I told you, you don't have to work. As long as you're here with me, I'll take care of you," Lyric told her, casting her eyes at Amber with a pleading look on her face.

Amber cared for Lyric a lot, but she was her own woman. She had to do what she had to do. Plus, all the madness that was going on wasn't on Amber's agenda to start with. She was at the right place, but at the wrong time.

"I'm gonna go and holla at Hollywood, so I can let her know what's up," Amber said, following Lyric out of the door.

"Call me before you leave," Lyric told her, disguising her anger with a forceful smile as she got inside of her drop top Thunderbird.

"Alright!" Amber said, leaning down kissing her on the forehead before walking towards the rental car that waited.

Lyric peered in her rearview mirror hoping Amber stayed instead of leaving. They both pulled off going their separate ways with thoughts of each other on their brains. Amber called Hollywood and told her she was on her way over. She hadn't talked to Hollywood in a few days, so she didn't know about the dispute she had with Redline. Amber made it to I-10 East in no time, thinking about her problems exiting Federal Road and Uvalde.

"This is the craziest shit I've ever been through in my life," Amber said to herself, rubbing her hand across her jawbone unconsciously.

She thought about how she almost lost her life in the house fire that Fast Blacc tried to barbecue her and Hollywood in. The hairs on the back of her neck stood up, as goose bumps began invading her body like illegal immigrants.

"Fuck this shit!" Amber thought to herself, with a daunting expression on her face knocking on Hollywood's front door.

(SOME PEOPLE HOPE FOR PEACE, BUT
MAJORITY PREPARE FOR WAR.)

CHAPTER 8

Redline sat at the dinner table stuffing his face full of French fries and fried fish. There was a sudden knock at the front door and Redline's hand blurred grabbing his .45 automatic from off of the table.

"Boy put that damn gun down, it's only Amber," Hollywood said, glancing at him with a strained expression on her face as she went to answer the door.

Redline didn't tell Hollywood about his near skirmish with death. He was fully aware the streets could be a deceitful enemy.

"Girl, I guess I made it just in time," Amber said, with her nose in the air sniffing like a hungry bitch. Amber followed Hollywood towards the kitchen as the aroma became stronger.

"Sit down girl, while I go and fix you a plate," Hollywood told her, walking back into the kitchen.

Redline peeped Amber swaying her hips towards the table. His dick tried to glimpse standing tall in his pants.

"'Nigga, why do you got that gun on the table?" Amber asked, sneering at the nickel plated .45 with a frozen expression.

"I'm just staying ready, that way I won't have to get ready. You feel me?" Redline stressed, licking the ketchup off his fingers. The sight of him licking his fingers made Amber's pussy immediately wet.

"I guess, if you say so," Amber responded, walking into the kitchen to wash her hands. Redline peeped at her butt as if it was calling his name.

"Your hungry ass just couldn't wait huh?" Hollywood asked, with a plate of French fries and fried fish in her hands.

"Bitch please, you act like this is Joe's Crab Shack or something," Amber joked, as she was washing her hands. They all sat at the dinner table enjoying their food, with their eyes stealing glances at each other.

"I ran into Fast Blacc today," Redline said, nonchalantly chewing on a piece of fish. Hollywood and Amber exchanged glances simultaneously with gaping looks on their faces.

"And when were you gonna tell me that?" Hollywood asked, with a poisonous glance.

Amber cast her eyes at Hollywood thinking, "He's telling you now bitch!"

"Look don't get to acting stupid. I only been here thirty minutes," Redline told her, with his dark pupils gleaming in her direction. Redline knew Fast Blacc was a sensitive subject with Hollywood. Therefore, he paused, selecting his words wisely.

"I went out there to Killeen to see what I could shake up. I don't know if the nigga was following me or not, but we met up," he explained, his eyes shining bright with malice.

Hollywood could see the gleam of deceitfulness in his eyes, as her eyes were glinting with anger.

"So that explains why you're walking around here with that," She said, pointing at the gun on top of the dinner table.

"What else happened?" Amber asked, shifting the conversation back on track. Redline broke down the rest of the story.

He thought it was strange how he ran into the exact person he went to Killeen looking for. The shady thoughts about Tron quickly disappeared, as his brain focused on Fast Blacc and how he tried to kill them both. Fast Blacc was causing too much havoc in his life, and he'd only been out of prison a month. But, one thing Redline did know, payback was a bitch by all means necessary. However, he was still leery when it came down to Hollywood.

He gazed at Hollywood and Amber discussing the events that took place with Fast Blacc. Redline thought about how he was acting irrational by having Amber and Hollywood together. He knew Amber was a down and loyal bitch, but he couldn't risk taking anymore gambles. It took him to many years to build up his trust with Hollywood, to let a few seconds of dumb thinking destroy it all.

"Look out Amber, when are you going back to work?" Redline asked, ignoring Hollywood's gaze upside his head.

"That's why I came over here. To tell y'all I was going back to work," Amber said, glancing at Redline - secretly lusting of eating him for dessert.

"What are you gonna do about Lyric?" Hollywood asked, snapping Amber out of her trance.

"Ain't too much I can do. I'm all about my money Hollywood, and all this gangsta shit is too much for me," Amber told her, glaring at the .45 automatic boring back at her.

Redline felt relieved when he heard Amber say she was going back to work. That was one less problem he had to worry about, because Amber held a secret, he didn't want Hollywood to find out.

(NO MATTER WHAT YOU DO, OR HOW MANY
TIMES YOU GET AWAY, YOU WILL NEVER
FOOL THE LORD.)

CHAPTER 9

"REAL NIGGAS WILL RIDE"
(BEN TAUB HOSPITAL)
HOUSTON, TEXAS

Redline woke up early the next morning and went to visit Flagg in the hospital. He missed his homeboy a lot. Redline had more love for Flagg than anyone in his own family. So, when he heard Flagg was shot, that ate away at his conscience. He gazed down at his homeboy who he has known since the early nineties. Redline thought back to the day Flagg told him to leave everything alone, until he was released from prison.

"There's no need for you to try and rush things, Hollywood ain't hurting for nothing she's doing good," Flagg said, as he exchanged places with Redline behind the sheet where they were hiding getting high. "You should be out in a year or two at the most. Your books are loaded up, so why take the chance of putting somebody in your business?" Flagg continued, as he peered in the small piece of mirror watching down the row for the Correctional Officers.

Redline sat on the toilet behind the sheet and listened to every word Flagg said, as he inhaled deeply on the good kush.

"I know how you feel though, cause my momma used to tell me all the time. Boy, you act like that money is burning a hole in your pocket," Flagg said, as he peered in the eye down the row.

Redline knew Flagg was looking out for his best interest, so he never interrupted him when he was dropping any type of knowledge his way. Redline absorbed everything just like a sponge. He looked up to Flagg like the big brother he always wanted, so he never disagreed with anything he told him. Redline never told Flagg about the stupidity he did behind his back. It was kind of hard to explain to the same person who advised him not to do what he did in the first place.

Redline snapped out of his daze when the door open. "Nice to meet you again. Sorry, but I forgot your name," Dr. Wilson said, walking over to him shaking his hand.

"It's Redline!" He told her, as they exchanged glances. "Say Doc, is there any way you can move my homeboy to a different room?" Redline asked, as he cast a glance in Flagg's direction.

Dr. Wilson sensed the worry and sincerity in his voice. "Is there a problem I need to know about?" She asked, with a concerned look.

"Not really, I just feel like he would be safer on another floor or something," Redline told her, unconsciously rubbing his hand over his face looking down at Flagg.

"I don't have a problem having Flagg moved to a different floor, but I would like to know the real reason why?" Dr. Wilson said, grasping Redline's undivided attention mentioning her patient by his alias name.

Redline's heart kicked up a few notches digesting what the doctor had said. "How do you know Flagg?" he wondered, with his heart hammering.

"I used to date his homeboy named T," She smiled, walking over to Flagg's bedside checking the flow of the IV, making sure the needle was secured within his vein.

"The dude you told us about last time wasn't a friend. I feel like the less you know the better off you'll be, you feel me?" He said, looking down at Flagg.

"I can understand that. I'll have him transferred to another floor. So, whenever you come back to see him, I'll be notified first," she said, walking towards the door.

"Say Doc, what's your name?" Redline wondered, curiously.

"N-Nika!" She told him pausing, after changing her mind stepping out of the room.

Redline grabbed Flagg by the hand and said a silent prayer for him.

"Talk to the man up above about whatever, and with faith, things will happen for you," Redline began batting away his tears. "GOD will make things work out for the best. Your enemy will face consequences and repercussions," Redline kissed Flagg on the top of his head and left out of the room feeling regretful.

(A PERSON WITH A LOT OF SO-CALLED FRIENDS, WILL LEARN IN THE END WHO IS A FRIEND. THAT PERSON WILL STAY DOWN CLOSER THAN A BROTHER.)

CHAPTER 10

"REVENGE IS A MUST"
(CITY LIGHTS)
KILLEEN, TEXAS

Tron received a call from Lil' Branon telling him to meet him at club City Lights. By the time he made it there the parking lot was jammed packed. The line to enter the club was stretching around the building. There were so many women of all shapes, sizes, and colors. Every one of them were dressed to impress smelling their best.

Tron parked his Porsche Boxster Spyder up front with the rest of the parking lot pimps, even though it was standing out like a black eye. He tipped the valet a Grant before walking to the front of the line. All eyes were on him walking by the Soul Train line of beautiful women. Tron was looking good, feeling good, and smelling good. He was tempted plenty of times to snatch up a beautiful woman and jump back in his car and leave.

His high school associate was the bouncer working at the front door, so he didn't have to wait in the long line. He showed Big Brick appreciation by slipping him a Grant while he was shaking his hand.

"What are you doing? Are you just going to walk in the club and leave me standing out here?" a sexy, light-complexioned female asked.

Tron turned around looking into the eyes of one of the women he had noticed when he walked past the line.

"I'm sorry baby! My mind is on cloud nine, so you know I'm floating," Tron said, grabbing a hold of her hand securing his arm around her waist walking into the club.

He glanced down admiring the sexy woman. She stood 5'4", weighing 125 pounds. Her ass was so fat, it had to weigh twenty five pounds all by itself. Her eyes were an alluring green.

"I'm glad you're a real playa, and a quick thinker on your feet," she said, with a smile easing across her face.

"What's your name Miss Lady?" Tron asked, scanning over her body looking for flaws.

"Well, my name was going to be Tina tonight. But since you kept it playa I have to do the same. My name is Jennifer," she told him, holding her hand out gazing up at him.

"I'm Tron," he replied, grabbing her silky soft hand with a devilish grin on his face. "So, this is how you get into clubs when you don't wanna wait in line?" Tron asked, reaching into his pocket to pay their way inside.

"No, I don't! And put your money away I got it," Jennifer said, peeping him up and down from head to toe.

Tron smiled at the way she was serving him, because he liked when a woman was straight forward.

"Look out baby! I don't mean to be rude, but I'm here on business," Tron told her.

"Well I'll just give you my number, and when you find time within your busy schedule call me," Jennifer told him, reaching for his cell phone entering her digits.

Tron smiled again walking off to meet up with Lil' Branon. He walked up the stairs to their usual spot in the back corner overlooking the dance floor. Lil' Branon was conversating on his cell phone, and by the smile he had on his face Tron knew he was talking to Ke Ke. Lil' Branon ended the call.

"What's the deal man?" Lil' Branon asked, shaking Tron's hand.

"Man, I got wind Fast Blacc headed back to H-Town," Tron said, undressing the females with his eyes as they strutted by seeking attention.

"When do you wanna flip down there?" Lil' Branon asked,

narrowing his eyes at the waitress approaching their table with a bottle of Cîroc on a tray.

"The guy at the bar sent this up to you gentlemen," she said, casting her eyes towards the bar.

Tron and Lil' Branon simultaneously turned their heads peering over the balcony towards the bar.

Redline sat at the bar sipping Grey Goose and cranberry juice, as his eyes were roaming his surroundings. He was sitting at the end of the bar facing the entrance, so he could see everyone that walked inside. The place was a social beehive, crowded closing into full capacity. On the wall above the dance floor, there was a big projection screen displaying a cartoon porno flick. Redline almost missed the sight of Tron when he stepped in.

He had his eyes glued on a short and sexy female strutting through, like she was a Victoria's Secret runway model. Redline looked up and saw Tron walking up the stairs. He also noticed the same female he was admiring had her gaze beaming on Tron too.

Redline caught the attention of many flagging the waitress down with a handful of Ben Franks (*hundred dollar bills*). He ordered a bottle of Cîroc and had it sent up to where Tron was sitting. Less than five minutes later, two heads popped up from behind the balcony's wall with their eyes grimly looking in his direction. Redline held his glass in the air motioning a toast before taking a sip. He didn't recognize the other person Tron met up with. Tron signaled with his hand for Redline to come up and join them.

Redline sliced his way through the crowd with his drink held high, trying his best to avoid the careless partygoers. Lil' Ke Ke, Bun B, Chauncy Chun, Big pokey, Z-Ro and Rednose were performing live on stage. Redline didn't know if Tron was going to be there, but when a few big name rappers held a concert in a small town such as Killeen, hustlers with money were known to show up and shine. The only thing Redline had on his mind was, could Tron help him find Fast Blacc.

"What's up playboy?" Tron asked, reaching out to shake Redline's hand as his gaze stole a glance at his iced-out pinky ring.

"Same shit different smell," Redline told him, exchanging glances with Lil' Branon.

"This is my nigga Lil' Branon. Lil' Branon this is Redline, the nigga I was telling you about," Tron said, introducing the two. "Thanks for the Cîroc my nigga," Tron told him, opening the bottle pouring him and Lil' Branon a stiff drink.

"'It ain't nothing. Real niggas do real things, you feel me?" Redline said, taking a seat as his gaze was following a female swaying her ass.

"Say, my bad for what happened at Denny's today," Tron apologized, enjoying the great taste of the Vodka bobbing his head to the sounds of Z-Ro.

"Man, I told you I wasn't trippin' on that shit. It ain't like you hit my ride," Redline said, as his eyes were stuck on a young female slowly swaying her body to the music.

"I'm not talkin' about your car pimp. I'm talkin' about that ho ass nigga Fast Blacc," Tron said, with anger changing his appearance in seconds.

"Yeah, we ain't feeling that grimy ass shit that nigga pulled. It's death before dishonor with us," Lil' Branon said, with a look that darkened his face like a black cloud.

"Say Tron, how do y'all know Fast Blacc anyway?" Redline asked, wondering how well Tron knew Fast Blacc, and what they had in common.

Tron had to assess his mode and think about that question himself. He remembered the day Ralo and Bug walked into the warehouse with Fast Blacc behind them. Ralo introduced Fast Blacc to Tron. Tron remembered nodding his head, because he wasn't the type to just mix with anybody. Before you knew it, Fast Blacc had things rolling bringing money to the table left and right.

"Tron, you alright my nigga?" Lil' Branon asked, bringing him out of his daze.

"Yeah I'm cool. I was just thinking about the day Ralo brought that cake ass nigga to our spot. Why are you so worried about Fast Blacc anyway?" Tron asked, as him and Lil' Branon beamed at Redline waiting for an answer. Redline knew this question was bound to come up soon or later. He sat there thinking about the secret only him and Fast Blacc knew. Redline thought back to the day of their phone conversation.

"What's up?" Fast Blacc answered.

"What the fuck do you mean what's up!?" Redline hollered into the phone as his jugular vein throbbed in his neck.

"Hold up nigga, you got me fucked up. You act like I owe you or something—pussy ass nigga. I don't owe you a mutha fuckin' thing," Fast Blacc told him, raising his voice as he growled into his cell phone. "I was doing your mutha fuckin' ass a favor, bitch made nigga ass," Fast Blacc stressed, as he walked around the room.

"I paid your dumb ass to do a mutha fuckin' job, so how in the fuck was you doing me a favor, huh? You took something so simple and turned it into some more shit. How could your simple-minded ass fuck something up so easy?" Redline asked, with a grim look on his face.

"Nigga, I ain't fuck up a mutha fuckin' thing. Ralo fucked it up," Fast Blacc replied, gritting his teeth in a rage.

"Ralo! Ralo! Why in the fuck did you get somebody that's dumber than you to handle your business?" Redline asked, yelling into the cell phone forgetting he was locked up in prison.

"Man for all I give a fuck, you can suck my mutha fuckin' dick. You paid me—to smoke a nigga. It don't matter who done it, as long as it got taken care of, fuck it. Fuck the dumb shit you're talkin' about," Fast Blacc said.

Redline regretted depending on a blockhead to handle his business for him. However, since he wasn't able to do things himself, he had to rely on someone.

"Look out, I'm gonna be straight up with y'all. I paid Fast Blacc to do a hit for me on this nigga named Pee Wee. I fronted Pee Wee twenty books while I was doing time. I felt like I could trust the nigga because he was my brother-n-law." Tron and Lil' Branon exchanged glances before focusing their attention back on Redline.

"I told my girl to give her brother my stash and let him handle the rest. I guess that fast money blew his head up, and he thought he couldn't be touched because I was locked up," Redline explained, as his gaze drifted down to the melting ice in his glass. "The nigga said fuck me! But the fucked-up part is, my homeboy was in the car too. Now he's lying in the hospital stuck in a coma. Fast Blacc's dumb ass got Ralo to handle the job for him."

Lil' Branon looked at Redline taking a swallow of Cîroc straight from the bottle, squeezing his eyes shut as it was burning a trail from his throat down to the pit of his stomach.

"Redline, man I remember that day Ralo brought that car to the warehouse. That stupid ass nigga jeopardized all of our freedom with that dumb shit," Lil' Branon said, with an angry expression on his face. Tron began moving nervously around in his seat.

"He was bumpin' something about another nigga in the car too. But I was trippin' on all the blood to really pay attention to what he was saying," Lil' Branon explained, as his mouth was curling into an unconscious sneer.

"Where's Ralo at?" Redline asked, jerking from his thoughts. "The nigga blew himself up in front of the warehouse. Somehow his dumb ass crashed into a parked truck and blew up," Tron said, pausing while gazing around at the women walking by. "Somebody killed my kinfolk Bug too. He was found in the warehouse with a hole in the back of his head. The police found a hoe dead with him too," Tron told him, pouring himself another drink unconsciously rubbing his goatee.

"My nigga, we been knowing each other for a good minute now. I know you been keeping it real with me all the way across the board. So, I can't do nothing but stay down and help you find the bitch made ass nigga," Tron said, exchanging a poisonous glance with Lil' Branon who was nodding his head up and down as a sign of approval.

"Well it's all understood then," Redline told them, holding his glass up for a refill. A crooked smile began creeping across his face.

"Revenge is a must!" Redline said, seeing the light of murder in their eyes. They all made a toast to revenge, each lost in their own murderous thoughts.

(SOME PEOPLE CHASE OTHERS THAT SHOULD BE LEFT ALONE. WHY CHASE THOSE WHO SHOULD NOT BE CHASED?)

CHAPTER 11

"NO HALF STEPPING"
(5th WARD)
HOUSTON, TEXAS

SHE KNOWS WHO I AM...Fast Blacc took another drag from the sherm becoming frenzy slowly exhaling. He scooped up a full extract bottle from a dope spot in Coke Apartments. The formaldehyde had his vision crystal clear and his hearing became sharper. Fast Blacc was creeping down Lockwood at a snails' pace. The four fifteen-inch speakers in his trunk were beating up the concrete.

Tupac had him in a trance that plenty of sherm heads have been in before...An OUT-OF-BODY experience. Fast Blacc was floating outside of his body looking down at himself driving down Lockwood. He felt like he was living, but his mind was registering that he was dead. He peered down at himself driving twenty-miles-an-hour under the speed limit. The limit was only thirty-five.

Everything around him, including the sky was smoke grey. He thought the world was about to end. Sweat was pouring down his face into his eyes causing them to burn. Cars were passing by him blowing their horns, which was to no avail. Fast Blacc didn't care about anyone, not even the police. Tupac didn't give a fuck either, as he screamed "HAIL MARY NIGGA!" Fast Blacc was so high he began begging Mary to bring him back down. He cried watching himself turn down Brackenridge Street.

Looking from above he saw Tiffany walking out of her house

towards his car. "Boy, what the fuck is wrong with you? Turn that shit down with your crazy ass," Tiffany said, shaking her head noticing he wasn't in his right mind frame.

She opened the car door and turned off the ignition before helping him into her house. He slowly began drifting back into his body.

"Thank you, LORD!" Fast Blacc said, acting like a burglar stole his brain away in pieces.

"Your mutha fuckin' ass need to be thanking me," Tiffany told him, shaking her head.

"Thank you, Holy Mary!"

Tiffany started laughing helping him over to the couch. She knew once he came down from his high, he would be back to normal. She walked in the kitchen pouring him a big glass of milk. She knew the milk would help him descend from his high.

"Here boy, drink this milk, Tiffany said, handing him the glass. I don't know how you're able to maintain smoking that shit every day."

Fast Blacc stared at her with a sneer on his face downing the glass of milk. Redline and Tron were the first ones to cross his mind. He pictured them standing in front of the Denny's restaurant in the midst of a conversation. He wondered what they were talking about? Just the thought of Redline and Tron together only made matters worse. Tron knew a little bit about him, but not enough for him to really worry about. Fast Blacc lined up his threats.

"Redline's ho ass gotta go. I can't forget that pretty bitch Hollywood. Tron also, along with Miss Stacks bitch ass," he laughed at his thoughts.

Fast Blacc compared the situation as being a game of chess. Every one of his moves had to be his best move.

"I'm the mutha fuckin' chess master. No Mistakes. No Mercy Nigga!" He said to himself, with a grim look on his face.

He labeled each one of his future victims as a chess piece, according to what he felt they were capable of doing. In the back of his brain there wasn't going to be any stalemates. His opponents would try their best to pursue a checkmate by any means necessary. Fast Blacc placed Hollywood as the Queen. She was very deadly and could move across the whole board quickly and precisely until she was dealt with.

He placed Redline in the King's position. Redline always stays put, and let others handle his dirty work. Fast Blacc knew this from experience the way Redline used him to kill Pee Wee. He knew Redline would defend with extreme skill if threatened. Lyric was a Knight. She would move indirect or diagonal, and she tends to escape her adversaries by a hair.

Amber was pin pointed as a Rook. She was always uncovered. Her only options were to go forwards or backwards, hoping she could side-step any problems. Tron was a knight too. He would seize the moment without causing direct confrontation but will attack. Fast Blacc didn't know if Lil' Branon was involved in the drama. If he was, he'd be labeled as a pawn in the game of death. Fast Blacc knew Lil' Branon would be somewhere in front of Tron. And as long as he doesn't move, he should be safe. Fast Blacc sat thinking about every person he was going to kill.

Tiffany was a true-blue bitch, so he planned on using her for his own benefits. He became aroused watching her walk around in a leopard print skirt, with a black Ralph Lauren cashmere blend top, and a pair of Black Christian Louboutin suede pumps. When it came down to looking fly, Tiffany was number one on Fast Blacc's list. Her thighs were screaming for attention as her skirt was sneaking up them slowly. He started stroking himself through his pants watching her ass jiggle with each step she took.

"I guess you're not to fucked up, sitting up there playing with that big ole dick," Tiffany said, eyeing him with a frozen expression.

"Tiff, baby you can make any nigga come down the way you're lookin'. Thanks for the milk. I needed that," He told her, with lust glinting in his eyes.

"I know what else you need too. It'll make your blood pressure go down, so you won't get a headache," she smiled, watching as he was playing with himself.

Tiffany paraded over in front of the couch, standing in front of him with her legs wide apart. She elevated her skirt, inching it along her thighs exposing more golden-brown flesh. When Fast Blacc saw her fresh Brazilian waxed kitty kat, he snatched his pants down to his ankles. His dick stood straight up like a flagpole. Tiffany raised one leg on the couch jack knifing two fingers into her shallow canal. She fingered her pussy while looking at Fast Blacc caressing his dick.

"Oooo boy, I'm about to cum," she moaned out.

Fast Blacc pulled her fingers out of her wetness licking her juices completely off. He leaned forward placing one of her legs over his shoulder, tongue diving into her sweet honey. Tiffany's whole body spasmed uncontrollably as Fast Blacc was skillfully bending corners with his tongue around her walls. She clutched the back of his head jamming his face in her pussy.

"Yeah that's it! Suck it like your momma's titty," Tiffany ordered him. "Oooo, Blacc I'm finna cum. Oooh! Mmmm, I'm coming," she yelled out, as her body instantly became weak. Fast Blacc continued to suck her dry, like he was an algae eater sucking on the inside of a fish tank. Tiffany couldn't pry him off of her brown sugar, so she held his nostrils closed making him come up for air. Working magic on her clothes, she quickly made them disappear, slamming her face into his lap. She loved the way his dick shined coated with her saliva. She already knew how many licks it took to make him blow up like the Challenger rocket. Fast Blacc pushed her off of his dick. He wanted to blast off deep inside of her tight pussy. He eased himself back on the sofa observing.

Tiffany worked herself down the length of his dick really slow, until it was all the way inside of her. He loved the sight of her round ass and pretty pussy coating his dick with nectar. Once Tiffany regulated herself around his full thickness, she placed her hands on the floor grinding vigorously in his lap. He stretched his legs straight out, grabbing her hips ramming his dick further into her pussy.

"AAAAAHH!" Fast Blacc grunted out, erupting deep inside of her as his toes began curling up. Tiffany rode his dick until it became flat. He didn't know which was going to kill him first. His enemies or pussy. The more he thought about it, he would love perishing away with a feeling like this. A smile worked its way across his face thinking about dying in some pussy.

(YOUR TONGUE CHOOSES WHETHER YOU LIVE OR DIE.)

CHAPTER 12

"GOING IN CIRCLES"
(610 LOOP)
HOUSTON, TEXAS

Lyric was driving to work unable to keep her thoughts off of Amber.

"How could she just up and leave me like this? Was everything she told me a lie? Who the fuck does she think I am?" Lyric thought to herself, with anger dimming her face like a murky cloud. "Got me lying up with her ass, like her pussy is made of velvet. What the fuck am I supposed to do?" she wondered, gripping the steering wheel.

So many speculations crossed her mind, she didn't even realize she was driving around in a circle on the freeway. This was her second trip around the 610 Loop. Lyric began beating on the steering wheel increasing her speed.

"Why me? What the fuck did I do wrong?" She hollered out.

Lyric called Hollywood in hope of finding information that would help her figure things out. Hollywood's phone went straight to the voice-mail. Lyric tried the number once again.

"Hey, this is Hollywood. If it's important leave a message, and I'll get back with you as soon as possible."

Lyric ended the call without leaving a message. Images of Hollywood and Amber began invading her brain.

"Could Amber be playing the both of us? I guess she thinks she can have her cake and eat it too," Lyric thought to herself, making her third trip around the 610 Loop with no plans of exiting on her mind.

She tried her best not to picture Amber and Hollywood twisted up like a pretzel enjoying each other's company. Lyric couldn't understand why she was so jealous of Amber when she had a girlfriend of her own. They say love makes a person do and say things without thinking. That was the situation in Lyric's case. She didn't give a damn about nothing. Only Amber. Her thoughts screamed, "AMBER! AMBER! AMBER!"

Lyric tried calling Amber. The call went straight to her voice-mail too. She threw her cell phone against the windshield exiting the freeway on a mission.

After her adrenaline rush there was no one to blame, but she was still mad. The only thing she had to face were the problems causing her pain. When a person is effusively disturbed, anger is the first emotion to rise to the surface. Then comes frustration. Once frustration sets in, along comes the schemes and wicked plots to get even. Love will make people do things they never have done before in their life; Lyric's heart was introduced to love at a young age when her mind wasn't fully developed. Seeking and wanting to be loved scared her for life.

(MANY PEOPLE CLAIM THEY HAVE UNCONDITIONAL LOVE, BUT CAN A FAITHFUL PERSON BE FOUND?)

CHAPTER 13

"TIME FOR REVENGE"
(5TH WARD)
HOUSTON, TEXAS

Fast Blacc and Tiffany were in the bathroom continuing another round in the shower. Fast Blacc threw all stiff jabs, boxing her pussy into the corner. Tiffany's knees wobbled as she began melting down the shower wall, out for the count. He washed up then went to get his mind right. That way he could plot out a solid and simple plan to succeed. Fast Blacc opened the extract bottle filled with formaldehyde. The fumes quickly charged his nose. He pulled out a More cigarette dipping it into the substance. He lit the cigarette.

(POOF!) Fast Blacc started laughing blowing the flame out. He inhaled at a worm's pace, closing his eyes as the effects of the drug quickly took over his brain.

(SHE KNOWS WHO I AM!) Those words jumped into his mind again. Fast Blacc might have been higher than the heavens, but he wasn't an idiot. He knew Miss Stacks had incriminating information on him and could ruin his plans before they were even started. Not too many women knew his real name, and if they did, they were carrying his child or filing child support against him. He wasn't about to let Miss Stacks send him back to prison, a place he vowed never to return to. She would have to die first.

"Boy, if that shit keeps your dick hard like that, you need to smoke the whole bottle," Tiffany told him, smiling as she was rubbing Palmers body lotion over her body.

"Say Tiff, I need for you to call this bitch job and find out if she's at work. And if they ask who you are. just tell 'em anything,'" Fast Blacc told her, flicking the ashes in the ashtray.

"She must have put that pussy on your ass, for you to be checking up on a bitch," Tiffany said, with a smirk on her face.

"N'all baby, it's far from that. I'm not weak behind no hoe. Pussy is the easiest thing to get on earth," He winked his eye taking a drag off of the sherm he was smoking. "I'm willing to bet you Tiff, that I could walk into any store and talk up on a piece of pussy. But if I was to walk into that same store and try to talk up on a cup of water. I'll be shit out of luck," Fast Blacc told her, watching her frown at his words.

"So that's how you feel about me? Just a piece of pussy?" she asked, with a venomous glare.

"If that was the case, I wouldn't have told you a mutha fuckin' thing. But n'all, I wanted to lace you up on the real. Now let's make this phone call-so I can find this bitch," he said, slapping her butt with a smile twitching at his mouth.

"Where does she work at?" she asked.

"She works for TDC at Coffield unit. Her name is Miss Stacks. Let 'em know she has a funeral to attend,"

"Her own," he thought to himself. Tiffany began searching for the information on the internet.

She got the number in a matter of minutes. She called and was told that Miss Stacks was not at work, and she was expected back from her vacation tomorrow. Tiffany ended the call relaying to Fast Blacc what she was told. He closed his eyes meditating on his thoughts.

(THE STRONG HEARTED WILL PLAY NO GAMES, OR BECOME A VICTIM TO ENEMIES.)

CHAPTER 14

"BACK ON THE GRIND"
(COFFIELD PRISON)
TENNESSE COLONY, TEXAS

Amber made it back to work, glad to be back on the hustling scene. "Hustle, Hustle, Hustle hard. Closed mouths don't get fed on this boulevard," she sung to herself, walking down the hallway trying to keep her mind off the numerous calls on her cell phone.

Amber was glad she only had to worry about horny inmates while at work. And the best thing about that was, she already knew what they wanted. So, if they weren't talking her kind of language, she never wasted her time.

Amber still couldn't overlook the drama she went through within the last month. The news Redline served her and Hollywood about Fast Blacc wasn't something she wanted to hear. She walked to the commissary window to make a small purchase before reporting to her duty post.

"What's happening Miss Stacks? I thought you quit since I ain't seen you around," Funk said, eyeing her up and down.

"N'all, I'm still here," she told him, just to be nice. Amber knew he was the type of nigga that tried to befriend, by telling everything that the next person was saving or doing. She knew every inmate had a hidden agenda; it was just a matter of time before they exposed it.

Funk was a nigga who always called himself looking out for her, and that made her wonder. Amber would've respected him more if he would have been straight forward, instead of telling her about the next man and who not to associate with.

"So, when are you gonna stop fuckin' with these nothin' ass niggas and roll with the punches?" Funk asked, ignoring the way she was flinching when he spoke.

"First of all! What I do is my mutha fuckin' business, and who I fuck with is my choice. If you wasn't worried about the next nigga so much, we could've been making money," Amber stressed, as her hazel eves bore into his. "But no, you want to talk down to the point, where you feel like it makes yourself look good."

"I was just trying to look out 'cause I cut for you," Funk said, narrowing his eyes down the hallway.

"Yeah right! If I was actually getting cut for real every time, I heard that line, I would have bled to death by now," Amber snapped, sneering rolling her eyes.

"Bitch, you been off work and come back acting all stuck up. What you been doing fucking all night?" Funk told her, with his eyes flashing anger.

"You see, that's what I'm talking about. Let it out ho ass nigga. You been holding that in all this time?" Amber said, as her nostrils flared up.

"Fuck you dirty booty ass bitch."

"Eat my pussy nigga!" Amber hissed, grabbing her bag of commissary heading to her duty post.

She felt Funk's eyes lusting over her body, so she gave him a little more to think about. Amber peered back at him slapping her ass. She usually didn't entertain hatefulness, but a lot was on her mind.

"Miss Stacks, what's your location?" a voice asked, over her walkie-talkie.

"B-side hallway," she said, taking a deep breath.

"Call 2791!" a voice replied.

"Roger that!" she said, walking to the nearest phone dialing the extension number.

"'Hello this is Miss Stacks." "You have a call; I'll transfer you over. Hold on please."

"Thank you," Amber said, already knowing in her mind who it was. "Hello! Hello!" Amber was greeted with a dial tone.

She shook her head dialing 2791 back.

"Hello," a lady answered.

"This is Miss Stacks again. Did the caller mention a name?" Amber asked, with a puzzling look on her face.

"Oh! I'm sorry, she said her name was Lyric!"

"Alright thank you," Amber said, hanging up the phone with a smile running across her face.

(DO NOT ANSWER A FOOL RUNNING HIS MOUTH...OR YOU WILL BECOME A FOOL LIKE HIM.)

CHAPTER 15

"NO TURNING BACK"
(KIM'S CORNER STORE)
TENNESSE COLONY, TEXAS

Tiffany hung up the pay phone getting back into the dopefiend rental car. The reek of formaldehyde raped her nostrils before she turned on the defrost eliminating most of the order.

"What did they say?" Fast Blacc asked, smoking himself to oblivion.

"They said she was there, but I hung up before she got on the phone," Tiffany told him, flicking the air condition switch to high.

Fast Blacc took another hit off the sherm closing his eyes against the smoke that was consuming him. Tiffany couldn't stand the sherm smoke, but Fast Blacc had her nose wide open causing her to overlook his major flaw. She respected his gangster so seriously it made her juices flow. Tiffany knew he couldn't be fully trusted. Fast Blacc didn't know Low Low called and informed her about what happened the day he was a victim to burglary. Low Low explained to her that someone had ripped him off for six bags of money. Fast Blacc played her as if she was a rookie.

"Some niggas just don't know when they got a live bitch on their team, until it's too late," Tiffany thought to herself, in the climate of her suspicion. Fast Blacc was helping her out a lot, so she kept her thoughts secret.

"Payback is a bitch!" she thought to herself smiling, reaching over rubbing his dick through his jeans.

"We got a bunch of time to kill. We might as well get a room and chill,'" Fast Blacc said, with his famous crooked sneer on his face.

"I'm cool with that! And it looks like your homeboy is cool with it too,'" Tiffany told him, pointing at the bulge in his jeans. Tiffany knew when the time came, she wouldn't have a problem dealing with Fast Blacc...so she thought.

(ANGRY THOUGHTS TURN INTO ANGRY ACTIONS, SO STAY COOL, CALM, AND COLLECTED.)

CHAPTER 16

"ON THE RIGHT TRAIL"
(ANTOINE AND PINEMONT)
HOUSTON, TEXAS

Tron and Lil' Branon were parlaying in Fat Freddy's Pool Hall waiting for Renee to show up. Tron met Renee at Harlem Nites strip club a couple of years ago. Once she found out Fast Blacc hustled in Killeen, that gave her an excuse to call Tron. However, she was really calling to find out about Fast Blacc and the status of his income.

"Do you think this bitch knows where to find him at?" Lil' Branon asked, drilling the six ball into the corner pocket leaving three balls remaining.

"Man, I can't promise you nothing, but we gotta start somewhere. I just knew the hoe used to fuck with Fast Blacc, so I gave her a call. And guess what?" Tron told him, inhaling slowly from the Black & Mild.

"What's that?" Lil' Branon asked, raising up from the pool table waiting for an answer.

"We in luck! The nigga was at her spot a week ago in Kelly Courts. I figured I could persuade her with some big faces and some of this Tony Montana," Tron said, knocking down one of the three remaining balls on the pool table.

"She might not be game with setting the nigga up."

"Shit, we got a 70/30 chance. You know how them hungry hoes

from the nickel (5TH WARD) are," Tron said, thrusting the two ball into the left-hand side pocket then scratching the cue ball.

"FUCK!" Tron said, hiding the flare of his anger. Lil' Branon began laughing.

"I done heard that plenty of times. Eight ball in the right-hand corner pocket," Lil' Branon said, tapping the cue ball with pure finesse.

He sat down sipping on his drink before the eight-ball dropped into the pocket. Tron stood there gazing at Lil' Branon as a pair of soft hands covered both of his eyes.

"Guess who?" Renee asked, brushing her breast against his back.

"By the way they feel. I say it's 36D," Tron said, with a slight grin on his face. Renee playfully hit him upside his head. "Renee, this is my homeboy Lil' Branon."

Lil' Branon nodded his head what's up before offering her a drink. They all sat at the table and got straight down to business.

"Now, let me get this straight. All I have to do is call you whenever I see him, nothing more and nothing less?" Renee asked, exchanging glances with both of them.

"It don't matter how you do it. You can fuck 'em suck 'em, just be ready to move around after you call me," Tron told her, sipping on a glass of Don Julio and cranberry juice looking over the rim of the glass.

"What's all in it for me?" she asked, just like Tron expected.

Lil' Branon counted out ten, hundred-dollar-bills, sliding them across the tabletop in front of Renee. Wasting no time, she scooped the money up stuffing it inside of her one size to small outfit.

"Now, are there any bonuses when I get the job done?" Renee asked, reaching her hand underneath the table caressing his dick.

(AN ADRENALINE REPLY AWAKES WITH RISK, AND
RENEE'S WAS PUMPING OVERTIME.)

CHAPTER 17

"DISTRACTIONS"
(COFFIELD PRISON)
TENNESSE COLONY, TEXAS

Amber called Lyric several times during her thirty-minute break, but there was no answer. So, as soon as she got off of work, Lyric was the first person she called. The line rang a couple of times before Lyric answered.

"Damn, I've been trying to call you all day. Your phone kept going straight to your voicemail. What's up with that shit?" Lyric growled into the phone without even saying hello.

"Look here Lyric. I told you I was headed back to work. I probably was on the plane when you called. Plus, my phone was in my bag anyway." Amber explained. glancing both ways before turning with the flow of traffic. "Anyway, your ass knew I was at work. You called up here this morning," Amber was becoming frustrated with Lyric and her silly games.

"I didn't call up there this morning, I called your cell phone," Lyric raised her voice.

"Well, I got a call from the front office. They said the caller's name was Lyric!" Amber said, exhaling heavily rolling her eyes.

"I don't give a fuck what they said. I didn't call up there looking for you," Lyric yelled.

"I guess they just lied on you huh?" Amber told her, increasing speed because of her anger.

"All you gotta do is check your phone, I'm not lying. I never called your job."

Amber peered down at her cell phone checking her incoming calls. She didn't see the blue Crown Victoria zip out in front of her. Amber raised her head up and saw the red light, but it was too late. (BAM!) She slammed into the back end of the Crown Victoria.

"FUCK, FUCK, FUCK! I don't need this shit!" Amber yelled out, with a grim look on her face. When she stepped out of her car the driver of the Crown Victoria was walking towards her.

"I'm so sorry, are you ok?" Amber asked, overcome by embarrassment and anger looking at the damage. "Let me get my phone so I can call the police," Amber said, shaking her head.

"We don't have to call anyone, it doesn't look that bad," The female driver replied, peeking at the slight fender bender.

"Well, at least let me give you my insurance information," Amber told her, peering at her real thoroughly.

"We can squash all this nothing, if you're down to hook up-with me and my boyfriend," The female driver hesitated, biting down on her bottom lip while placing a hand on her hip. "That's him on the passenger side. Go check 'em out, he's cute!" She said, following behind Amber approaching their vehicle. The door opened slightly.

(EVIL THOUGHTS CAN BLOW UP INTO VICIOUS ACTS, WHICH CAUSES SUFFERING TO MANY.)

CHAPTER 18

"OLDEST TRICK IN THE BOOK"
(KIM'S CORNER STORE)
TENNESSE COLONY, TEXAS

F ast Blacc and Tiffany were sitting on the side of Kim's corner
store in a blue Crown Victoria with tinted windows. He broke
down his plan again to Tiffany. He didn't need any more dumb
mistakes when the plan was so simple. Fast Blacc noticed the slight
change in the flow of traffic.

"Get ready to roll out," he said, peering further down the street
trying to locate Miss Stacks car.

"NO MISTAKES NO MERCY NIGGA!" Fast Blacc thought to
himself, taking a hit off of the sherm then resting it in the ashtray. He
saw Miss Stacks coming down the street.

"That's her right there! Hurry up and pull in front of her," he
ordered, with his dark pupils gleaming at Miss Stacks car. Tiffany
maneuvered the big body Crown Victoria in front of her car. The stop
light was green in the turning lane leaving away from the unit. Tiffany
smashed on the brakes bracing herself for the impact.

The screeching tires were the first thing heard before the crash.
(BAM!) Fast Blacc laughed reaching for the sherm that fell into the
bottom of the ashtray. Tiffany hopped out of the car transforming into
an actress.

"OH MY GOD! Are you alright?" Tiffany asked, with a worried
expression on her face.

"Yeah, I'm ok. Let me get my phone and call the police," Miss Stacks said, shaking her head surveying the damage to her car.

"There's no need for that, it doesn't look that bad," Tiffany told her, trying her best not to glance back at Fast Blacc.

"Well, at least let me give you my insurance information," Miss Stacks said, gazing at Tiffany entirely.

"We can squash all this nothing if you're down to hook-up with me and my boyfriend," Tiffany said hesitantly, biting down on her bottom lip seductively placing a hand on her hip. "That's him on the passenger side. Go check him out girl, he's cute," Tiffany encouraged her, following her over to the passenger's side of the car.

The door opened up and Fast Blacc was pointing his gun right at her. Miss Stacks had a surprised look frozen on her face. Tiffany pressed the .380 she was carrying roughly in the spine of her back.

"Hello Amber! I mean Miss Stacks," Fast Blacc said, sneering. He popped open the trunk stepping out of the car. He glanced around making sure there wasn't any traffic or witnesses. Fast Blacc swung the gun down across Amber's head biting down on his teeth in anger. Tiffany grabbed her before she fell down, groaning under the weight. Fast Blacc quickly threw her into the trunk. They got back into the car with Fast Blacc behind the wheel.

"NO MISTAKES NO MERCY NIGGA!" His thoughts screamed out, narrowing his eyes at Tiffany. They drove back to H-Town and Fast Blacc had his mind on one thing. Disposing of the trouble in the trunk, once and for all.

(THOSE WHO CONTROL THEIR ANGER LIKE A DRIVER CONTROLS A SPEEDING CAR, THEY ARE THE ONES WHO ARE RUNNING THINGS. OTHER PEOPLE ARE JUST HOLDING THE STEERING WHEEL.)

CHAPTER 19

"UNPROTECTED SEX"
(ST. JOSEPH'S PROFESSIONAL BUILDING)
HOUSTON, TEXAS

"I don't know what the fuck she's talking about. I called her job!" Lyric said to herself, with both hands on the steering wheel swaying her neck glaring straight ahead. "I don't know who the fuck she thinks she is, talking about I'm calling her job. Like I'm the only one who knows where she works at," Amber had Lyric's mind in a tight clamp like a pair of vise grips. Lyric was heading to the St. Joseph Professional building off of Interstate-45 in the downtown area. She noticed her period was two weeks late, so she scheduled an appointment to see her personal doctor. Being pregnant ran around her mind like a two-year-old who had too much sugar. Fast Blacc was a lunatic she wished she had never laid eyes on.

"Damn, how can one nigga ruin my life so fast?" She thought to herself. "GOD please don't let me be pregnant by this nigga." Lyric pulled into the parking lot of the Professional building.

It was a beautiful sunny day, but Lyric was feeling partly cloudy. The clouds and the sun were reflecting off of the mirror tinted windows of the building. She parked her car thinking about the situation she got herself into.

"My period has never been late. Damn, I hope I'm not pregnant," she thought to herself, blowing air out between her lips gazing up at the clouds floating by.

Fast Blacc was the only man she slept with in the last two years. Her brain was strongly stuck on him being the reason for this visit. Lyric gripped the steering wheel tightly with both hands making her knuckles turn white. Goose bumps began marching up her arms and the back of her neck. She stepped out of her car activating the alarm. Lyric glimpsed up at the sky inhaling deeply.

"Bless me LORD!" She said to herself. exhaling walking towards the entrance doors.

It was a mid-day afternoon, and there weren't many people in the lobby. Lyric pressed the arrow pointing up waiting for the elevator. The wait wasn't long before she stepped on the elevator with a woman and her child following behind her. Lyric pressed the tenth-floor button.

"Can you please press the fourteenth floor," The woman asked politely. "Thank you!" Lyric pressed the button.

"You're welcome," Lyric said, glancing down at the little girl flashing back to her childhood.

The bell chimed indicating it was her floor. Lyric stepped off of the elevator walking to her doctor's office. There was only one person waiting to be seen, and that was a good sign to Lyric since the wait wasn't going to be long. So, she thought. "I'm here to see Dr. Howard."

"May I get your last name please?" the receptionist asked.

"It's Davenport," Lyric told her, glancing down at the paperwork. The receptionist ran her index finger down her paperwork stopping on Lyric's name.

"Ok, will you come in the back please." Lyric walked through another door and more goose bumps stood at attention over her body.

"Follow me please," a nurse said nicely.

Lyric followed the nurse leading her to an examining room. "Here's a gown, you can change in the restroom. The doctor will be with you in a moment," the nurse said, before walking off.

Lyric watched as she left out of the room. "Oh well, let's get this shit over with," she mumbled to herself.

She quickly changed into the gown sitting on the examining table. The Doctor came in taking care of his business with the least talk as possible. He was in and out less than ten minutes to retrieve her results. Tears began swelling in her eyes. She could never accept having

Fast Blacc's baby, not in this lifetime. Lyric closed her eyes thinking about her first murder (MONA) which wasn't planned. But in this case, if she was pregnant this murder would be premeditated. The child had to go. There were no ifs, ands or buts about it. Just like her first killing it threatened her livelihood. The Doctor opened the door holding her Pap test and pregnancy results.

"Miss Davenport, all of your tests came back good. You're one healthy woman. But you have to be a little more careful with your body. You're pregnant!" Dr. Howard revealed to her.

Those words echoed through Lyric's ears, making everything else around her shut down. The words "YOU'RE PREGNANT!" kept replaying over and over in her head.

"I'm pregn-!" Lyric tried to say pregnant, but she became dizzy passing out.

Dr. Howard has been Lyric's physician for over ten years, and he also knew her sexual preference. He checked her results twice before bringing her the news. Dr. Howard knew the child would be just another number on the abortion chart. The Doctor shook his head thinking. The high cost for a low living, death of the innocent. He felt Lyric wasn't going to let this child have a chance to breathe the air of this earth. Lyric was having visions of herself pulling into the parking lot. She saw herself getting out of her car looking up at the clouds floating by on the mirror tinted windows of the Professional building. Fast Blacc's face emerged from the clouds and covered the entire side of the building. Lyric ran inside right into a security guard.

"Excuse me ma'am, are you ok?" the security guard asked.

"Yeah, I'm ok," Lyric told him, before looking up into his face.

She screamed when she looked at the security guard and saw Fast Blacc. She ran towards the elevator and got on. There was a lady and a little girl on the elevator when she ran inside.

The little girl pressed number fourteen. "Can you please press number ten?" Lyric asked, glancing down at the little girl. The little girl pressed number ten.

Lyric stepped off of the elevator on the tenth floor. She turned around to thank the little girl for pressing her floor. Lyric saw the lady smiling holding onto the little girl's hand. Lyric looked at the little girl terrified. It wasn't a little girl. The child had Fast Blacc's face.

"You're welcome," he said sneering, flashing a mouthful of diamonds as the elevator doors closed.

Lyric regained consciousness raising herself up slowly. "Are you ok?" Dr. Howard asked, peering into her eyes.

"Yeah, I'm ok. I just got dizzy that's all," Lyric told him, adjusting her gown covering up her thick thighs.

"I prescribed you a little medication to calm your nerves and help you relax. You need to get a lot of rest. I rescheduled you another appointment for next week, we'll talk more then," Dr. Howard explained, before walking out of the room. Lyric already had a plan for the baby growing inside of her.

(ANYONE WHO DOES SHADY SHIT WILL BE REPAID FOR THEIR SHADINESS. THERE IS NO DISCRIMINATION.)

CHAPTER 20

"CHECKING IN"
(PAROLE OFFICE)
HOUSTON, TEXAS

Redline and Hollywood were sitting in the parole office on Telephone road waiting for his name to be called. Redline glanced around at all of the ex-offenders waiting to report in. Hollywood was shifting around in her seat uncomfortably like she had ants in her pants.

"Jones!" Mrs. Walkerson called out.

"About time! We been here long enough," Hollywood complained, with an impatient look on her face. Redline shook his head smiling at her as he was walking away.

Mrs. Walkerson was sitting behind her desk sorting through some paperwork in front of her when he walked in. Redline felt her eyeing him up and down taking a seat. Mrs. Walkerson was 5'6", weighing a hundred-twenty-five pounds. Her complexion was a paper sack brown. Her teeth were so white and straight, they could've been on a box of Colgate. She had a smile that would force you to sit down and get to know her better. Her perfume was captivating, drawing you in, making you want to violate her personal space. Mrs. Walkerson wore spectacles which gave her a sophisticated elegant look. Like always, Redline was so caught up in her beauty and finesse he didn't hear her talking to him.

"Jones! Jones!" She called out, waving her hand in front of his face trying to get his attention.

Redline rubbed his hand over his face. "My bad Mrs. Walkerson, I just zoned out."

"Wherever your mind was at, it must have been a nice place. Maybe you can take me there sometime," she said, with a smile on her face opening up his file.

Before Redline even had a chance to respond with something cunning, she was back to business.

"Are you ready to submit your urine sample?"

Redline's heart began pounding like an African war drum. "I asked are you ready to give me a urine sample?" she repeated, looking directly into his eyes folding her hands neatly in front of her.

Redline didn't know what to tell her, he'd been getting high since his last visit.

"No, I'm not ready," he told her, narrowing his eyes.

"Alright! Make sure you have yourself straight by the second of November," she said, glancing up from her paperwork.

"Thanks a lot!"

"No problem. Just don't disappoint me and go back to prison," she told him, picking up her glasses placing them back on her face. "Are you trying to find a job?" Mrs. Walkerson asked, without raising her head up from the paperwork she was filling out.

"I got a job, trying to find Fast Blacc's ho ass," he thought to himself. "I turned in a few applications here and there, nothing to brag about," he lied.

"I'm going to place you in Project Rio. They'll help you find a job. Plus, it's a good look if you decide to trip out," she said, with her head down peering over the top of her glasses. "It'll be twice a month for three months; you should have a job by then."

Redline glared at her nodding his head. He knew she was backing him real tough.

"You'll have a home visit on the tenth of next month, so don't have me waiting. I'll call when I'm on my way," she told him.

"Ok! Is there anything else I need to do?" Redline asked, watching as she was about to say something before changing her mind.

"No, that's all for today. Thanks for coming Mr. Jones," she said, extending her hand out to shake his. Redline shook her hand noticing how moist her palm was.

He smiled to himself walking out of the office. He felt her eyes again. He stopped before closing the door.

"You know lusting may not be a crime, but it's a sin," he told her. Mrs. Walkerson's face momentarily flushed. Redline closed the door and left.

Hollywood wasn't in the lobby when he stepped out, so he figured she was waiting outside in the car. He walked outside and the sun instantly began beaming on his face. A light breeze was blowing. Redline took a deep breath thanking the Lord for his freedom while walking to the car. Being free was a wonderful feeling and Redline didn't want to trade it in for anything in the world. He knew retaliation against Fast Blacc was a one-way ticket to the penitentiary, but he was ready for the ride, even though it meant going against his own word.

"Gotta do what I gotta do," he said to himself, looking at Hollywood reclining back in the passenger seat.

He opened the door, and before his ass touch the leather seats. "It took you long enough. If I didn't know any better, I would of thought you two were in there fucking. Are you fucking your parole officer?" Hollywood asked, trying to prevent the smile from creeping across her face.

Redline glanced and saw the pretty smile on her face. He leaned over softly kissing her on the lips. Their next stop was the hospital. Ben Taub was one place that was always busy twenty-four hours a day, seven days a week. Hospitals were like the streets, they never slept. Redline hadn't been back to see his homeboy since he asked Dr. Wilson to move Flagg to another floor for his safety. There was a young female intern working behind the counter moving quickly and efficiently.

"May I help you sir?" she asked, politely.

"I need for you to call Dr. Wilson and tell her Wilbert Hunter has a visitor," Redline told her. Hollywood glanced at him questioningly.

"I'll page her now. Please take a seat," she said, pointing to the waiting area. Redline and Hollywood found a seat luckily, sitting down.

He enlightened Hollywood on what he asked Dr. Wilson to do, and why. Redline and Flagg have known each other for too long, so he wasn't about to let their enemy have his way with his homeboy. Dr. Wilson arrived ten minutes later verifying the visitor like she promised. Redline and Hollywood took the elevator up to the fifth floor. Hollywood peeked at him as they rode up in silence. She wondered how long it was going to take to find Pee Wee's killer. She wasn't going to rest until his death was avenged. Hollywood played her cards like she was an amateur. An amateur was least expected to do certain things.

"Real killers move in silence," she thought to herself, stepping off of the elevator.

The thought of Redline having dealings with Fast Blacc never left her mind. Some things stuck with her like her A B C's, making it hard to forget. Her common sense was telling her one thing, but her mind was failing to accept the truth. Hollywood was refusing to let her better judgement play tricks on her. Playing dumb and lame was a totally different ball game, something she did really well.

Redline held the door open and they walked into the room. Flagg was lying in bed without any tubes crawling in his mouth and nostrils. He was even looking better despite his weight loss. Someone also took the time and shaved his face, making him look presentable. Redline said a silent prayer for his homeboy. He made it his duty to pray for Flagg every day, along with asking for forgiveness for his own actions.

"Give GOD all your problems my nigga. He's the only one who will have your back no matter what. I can't explain it, but things happen for crazy reasons. And only GOD can give you the answer," Redline said, gripping Flagg's hand blinking away tears before they fell down his cheeks.

Hollywood was sitting in a chair behind him listening to his every word. She said a silent prayer too, for her brother Pee Wee.

"There's a time and place for everything. A time to play dumb. A time to be smart. A time to fight. A time to run. A time for bullets to fly. A time for a nigga to bleed. A time for the guilty to beg for their life on their knees. GOD will help us Wee Pee," Hollywood said silently, looking at Redline in the disturbance of suspicion.

Reality began staining Redline's brain as he stood there watching Flagg with his fury well hidden. His conscience was working tougher than a construction worker, and Hollywood was the forewoman watching his every move. Redline was feeling her thoughts, and none of them were pleasant. He was getting tired of making excuses for not handling his business. It was time to put his plan into effect before Hollywood began putting the pieces to the puzzle together. The more he thought about Fast Blacc the higher his blood pressure started rising.

"I'll get back with you my nigga. It's time for me to put an end to this bullshit, or die trying," he said to himself, knowing his time was limited with all thinking and no action.

Redline and Hollywood were heading back home. He was so lost in his thoughts, Hollywood felt like something was wrong.

"What's wrong baby?" she asked, before he had the chance to gain control of his thoughts.

"Ain't nothing, just thinking," he said, hoping Hollywood wouldn't push the issue.

"Baby, you're doing some heavy thinking, cause I can hear your thoughts screaming from a distance."

"Hollywood don't worry. I got everything under control," he told her, without thinking about what he just said.

"You got what under control baby? What are you talking about?" Hollywood asked, turning in her seat facing him. "Are you talking about Fast Blacc?"

This was the first time Fast Blacc's name came up in a direct question without any speculations between them. Redline glanced at her nodding his head.

"Yeah!" He said, truthfully.

"Have you heard anything else about him?" Hollywood asked, with her eyebrows raising.

"Not yet. But I got a few ears in the streets, so hopefully something will turn up," Redline told her, glancing in the rearview mirror.

"If something does turn up I wanna be the first one to know, ok?"

Hollywood stressed, with malice spreading across her face. Redline felt her pain. He knew the loyalty she had for the ones she loves. He had to be careful, because any minor mistake could be deadly.

"Baby, you'll be the first one to know anything. I know how much you loved Pee Wee." Redline told her, turning on his signal light merging over in the right lane exiting the freeway on Federal Road.

Hollywood nodded her head expressing herself to the words her man was speaking.

"I just want you to have faith in your man and let me handle my business. You hear me?" Redline said, assessing his mood.

(YOU CAN GET AWAY FROM THE EYES OF OTHERS, BUT THE MAN ABOVE CAN SEE AND KNOWS ALL.)

CHAPTER 21

"NO TIME FOR MISTAKES"
(5TH WARD)
HOUSTON, TEXAS

ast Blacc and Tiffany completed their task without any problems. This was Tiffany's first time being involved in a kidnapping. The only good thing was she didn't have to worry about being caught after today. She cut her eyes at Fast Blacc driving the car smoking sherm after sherm, lost in his own world. Fear of being harmed began streaming through her mind for the first time since she met him. She was scared. Fast Blacc was beginning to look and act more like a zombie each minute passing. The closer they got to her house the more relaxed she became.

"I swear, after today, I'm not fucking with this crazy mutha fucka. I'm glad I didn't tell him I was pregnant," Tiffany said to herself, looking out of the passenger window.

"What did you say?" Fast Blacc asked, exhaling the sherm smoke through his nostrils.

This was his first time speaking to her since they threw Amber in the trunk of the car.

"I didn't say anything," Tiffany said, eyeing him swallowing her fear. "Lord, I promise you this is my last time messing with a wet head," she said to herself, staring blankly out the window.

Little did she know, this was her last time socializing with anyone period. A smile wormed across her face as they turned down Bracken-ridge pulling into her driveway. Tiffany jumped out of the car so fast she almost fell down. Fast Blacc's eyes bore in her direction with a vacant expression on his face.

"Say sexy black, I'll call you tomorrow sometime alright," Tiffany told him, closing the car door putting as much space as she could between the two of them. Fast Blacc nodded his head watching as she stepped into her house.

"NO MISTAKES NO MERCY NIGGA!" he said, dunking a cigarette into the almost empty extract bottle of formaldehyde.

He pulled the filter out of the end of the cigarette with his teeth. Each sherm he smoked made him feel like it was his first-time smoking. It was a feeling so wonderful. Even though he begged GOD plenty of times to help him come down from his high, and promised to never smoke again, a few hours later he was right back at it. Fast Blacc inhaled deeply holding his breath becoming lightheaded. Instantly, homicidal thoughts began engulfing his brain.

Tiffany was happy she made it home safely. As soon as the door closed her legs turned into noodles. She slid down to the floor with her back resting against the front door.

"Thank you, Lord, I'm through fucking with that crazy mutha fucka," she said, blowing air between her lips.

Tiffany locked her front door then stripped out of her clothes throwing them into the trash can. She walked into the bathroom preparing herself a hot bubble bath. Tiffany had been attracted to thugs ever since she was a teenager. But, never in her wildest dreams did she think she would become infatuated with a homicidal maniac. She dropped a few scented beads into her bath water watching them quickly dissolve. Tiffany eased herself down into the steaming hot water until it reached the bottom of her chin. The soothing hot bubble bath and scented beads instantly began easing her mind and relaxing her muscles. She closed her eyes drifting off to sleep.

Fast Blacc finished smoking his sherm. He popped open the trunk stepping out of the blue Crown Vic. He reached into the trunk grabbing a pair of gloves and a crowbar, then walking to the back of Tiffany's house. He began smiling when he saw the glass patio sliding door, because he knew it was easy for a burglar to gain entry. And Fast Blacc was a burglarizing veteran. He used the crowbar prying the patio door open with ease.

The sweet scent of flowers was the first thing he smelled before even crossing over the threshold. The fragrance alone was arousing his nature. The thought of Tiffany's fear and the element of her surprise had his blood pumping. He gripped the crowbar tightly as sweat was dripping down his face. The sweet aroma became stronger each step he took. Fast Blacc noticed a light peeking from underneath the bathroom door. He wasted no time at all. He slowly, quietly, and carefully began turning the doorknob. He inched the door open carefully. Through the bathroom mirror he peered at Tiffany laying in the bathtub. Her head was resting up against the wall, so Fast Blacc figured she was sleep.

Soundlessly he snailed the door open further. Within three noiseless steps he was standing over her sneering. Looking down at her caused rapid blood flow between his legs. Fast Blacc started fondling himself through his pants. Turning, he caught a glimpse of himself in the mirror.

"NO MISTAKES NO MERCY NIGGA!" his reflection whispered. Fast Blacc turned around raising the crowbar over his head.

"Don't nothin' come to sleepers but a dream bitch!" he hollered out, startling Tiffany from her sleep.

Once her mind registered on Fast Blacc face; she began screaming. Her scream was cut short as the crowbar came swinging down with brute force into her face. Blood gushed out rapidly. Tiffany didn't stand a chance upon each blow that was being delivered. Blood sprayed on the wall with each swing.

Fast Blacc looked down at her body submerging beneath the bloody red water. He snatched up a towel wiping the blood from his face. Fast Blacc had only one thing on his mind, and that was the process of elimination. His next victim...Lyric! She was the main reason he was tackling the situation he was up against.

"Loose lips, loose lips," he said to himself, walking out of her house. He hopped in the dope fiend rental car driving off into the night.

(WHY DO YOU HAVE A MOUTH IF YOU CAN'T BE HEARD?
WHY DO YOU HAVE EARS IF YOU CAN'T HEAR? WHY DO
YOU HAVE LEGS IF YOU CAN'T WALK? WHY DO YOU
HAVE A NOSE IF YOU CAN'T SMELL? WHY DO YOU HAVE
EYES IF YOU CAN'T SEE? WHY...BECAUSE YOU'RE DEAD.)

CHAPTER 22

"ON THE MOVE"
(US 59 NORTH)
HOUSTON, TEXAS

Tron and Lil' Branon became tired of waiting around for something to transpire. They split up to cover more ground. Renee dropped a bug in Tron's ear informing him that Fast Blacc was always in the strip clubs off of I-45 South. She also told Tron she needed a ride home from work. Tron knew what the super freak wanted, and his mind was far from getting his dick wet.

"Look here Renee, I'm a shoot Lil' Branon your way he'll take you to the house. I'm finna hit up the strip clubs and see what's jumpin'," Tron told her, glancing in his side mirror changing lanes.

"Tron, I'm not the type of bitch to be sweating no nigga for no dick. I get what I want," Renee said, with an attitude.

"Well, I guess we both are the type who get what we want. Right now, I want that nigga Fast Blacc. So, the rest of that bullshit can wait, you hear me?" Tron told her, with his mouth twisting in anger.

"When are you sending your homeboy to pick me up?" she snapped.

"As soon as you tell me where you work at."

"I work at Roxy's on South Post Oak. Just give him my number in case he gets lost."

"Alright, I'll hit you up later on," Tron said, with his face cracking into a smile.

"Yeah, whatever!" Renee told him, ending the call.

Tron called Lil' Branon and the line began ringing before the voice mail picked up.

"Where the fuck is this nigga at?" Tron said to himself, dialing the number again.

"What's up my nigga?" Lil' Branon answered, turning down the screwed and chopped Slim Thug CD he was jamming.

"Where are you at?" Tron asked.

"I'm in South Park right now, bouncin' in and out of these after hours," Lil' Branon said.

"Anybody seen that nigga?" Tron asked, exiting I-45 South

"I ran across a few niggas, but they said they ain't seen him in a while."

"I need you to go and scoop Renee up from work, while I swing through these clubs off of 45."

"Where does she work at?" Lil' Branon asked, nodding his head to the music.

"She works at Roxy's on Post Oak."

"Bet that! I'll holla back your way when I drop the bitch off," Lil' Branon said.

"Keep your eyes open and be careful my nigga, you hear me?" Tron told him, exiting the freeway on Howard and Belfort.

"I got you pimp," Lil' Branon said, ending the call.

Tron thought to himself how things went from him having money, moving kilos, to his cousin Bug getting killed, and Fast Blacc shooting at him and Redline. Now he was on the hunt for his victim seeking his own form of justice. A strange feeling came across him. Tron shook off the strange feeling lighting up a chocolate blunt filled with some topflight weed he copped from his homeboy Rufus. He stopped at the first strip club he saw.

(THE MIND ALWAYS FLASHES BACK TO CERTAIN TIMES WHEN WE SHOULD HAVE ACTED IMMEDIATELY. IN OVERALL REALITY, IF WE WOULD HAVE FOLLOWED OUR FIRST THOUGHT, A LOT OF MISTAKES COULD HAVE BEEN AVOIDED.)

CHAPTER 23

"MONEY TALKS"
(ROXY'S STRIP CLUB)
HOUSTON, TEXAS

A slow smile began crawling across Fast Blacc's face when Renee ended the call on her cell phone. When she left Tron and Lil' Branon at Fat Freddy's, she called Fast Blacc and told him what they were planning. Renee felt by telling Fast Blacc what was going on he was going to break her off with some money.

"Now I handled my end, make it rain on me baby," Renee told him, not really knowing she just cut a deal with the devil.

Fast Blacc sneered, sliding twenty-five hundred-dollar bills across the table. Renee snatched up the money like someone was trying to beat her to it. She put the money in her bra with the rest she had made throughout the night.

"Say sexy, you know you can take my word to the bank. If I say it, it's as good as done," Fast Blacc said, exchanging glances with her before looking around the club.

"Do you need me to do anything else?" Renee asked, batting her eyelashes rapidly.

"N'all, you already did enough. I don't want you to feel like I'm trying to use you."

"Boy, you know we better than that. And if it's some money to be made, you can always count on me," Renee said, rubbing her foot up and down his leg underneath the table.

"I'm feeling you on that. So, when I run across something else, I'll fuck with you," Fast Blacc told her, taking a sip from his drink.

"Alright then! Let me go finish my last set before my ride gets here," Renee said, slipping her feet back into her high heels.

She stood up walking away swaying her ass with each step she took.

Fast Blacc didn't know why he liked Fifth Ward hoes so much. He didn't entertain that thought for long, as he watched Renee's ass cheeks jiggle. He shook his head walking out of the club. Fast Blacc knew the game really well, especially when it came down to grimy, sneaky, scandalous, cum drunk bitches.

He walked back to the dope fiend rental car he was riding in. He reached underneath the seat for his pistol tucking it in his waistband. He grabbed a rag from off the floorboard wiping everything down, even places he knew he didn't touch. After wiping the door handles and the trunk, he threw the keys along with the rag into the dumpster. Pulling his fitted cap down low to conceal his face, he adjusted his shirt hiding the .380 Glock he was carrying. He walked over to the Metro bus stop in front of the club. He wanted to have a bird's eye view of everybody coming and going. He picked up an old Green sheet newspaper off the ground and fronted like he was reading.

Fifteen minutes later Lil' Branon was turning into the parking lot. Fast Blacc watched the Dodge Stratus reverse into a parking spot, a couple spaces over from the abandoned Crown Vic. He gazed at the Dodge Stratus for five minutes before Lil' Branon hopped out walking inside the club. Fast Blacc couldn't believe his luck. Lil' Branon had committed a rookie mistake like the amateur he was. Fast Blacc looked around then made his move towards the car Lil' Branon left running. He opened the back door and a cloud of smoke rushed into his nostrils. The white cloud of smoke was escaping from the car at a fast pace. Fast Blacc jumped into the backseat closing the door behind him. He peeked around to see if he was noticed by anyone. No one saw him get into the car but the slow burning blunt sitting in the ashtray.

He took a couple of hits off of the blunt loading one into the chamber. He lay on his back across the floorboard of the backseat with his head resting against the back door. The .380 was camouflaged with the darkness of the night, aiming at the driver's seat. Fast Blacc exhaled the smoke really slow, waiting. Seconds turned into minutes which seemed like hours as nervous sweat began dripping from his face. His heart hammered against his chest making him wonder if they would hear it.

"Boy, you got it smelling good up in here," Renee said, licking her lips.

"Damn, you don't waste no mutha fuckin' time, do you? You ain't even put your seatbelt on, and you already trying to wrap your lips around something," Lil' Branon joked.

Renee rolled her eyes reaching for the seatbelt.

"Where do you stay at?" Lil' Branon asked, turning left on S.Post Oak.

"I stay in Kelly Courts. Do you know where that's at?" Renee snapped, with an attitude working her neck.

Lil' Branon reached for the blunt in the ashtray. "Yeah, it's in the Nickel off of I-10," he said, lighting the blunt back up.

Lil' Branon quickly noticed the end of the blunt was wet with saliva, something he couldn't stand. It was also something he couldn't understand since he was the only one smoking it.

He shook his head and tore the end off, passing it to Renee. "Here you go, you can't find this in Kelly Courts," Lil' Branon joked.

"Nigga, I ain't doing no trippin'. We can go get a zone from my puntas off Crane Street," Renee told him, raising her voice.

"Girl shut up! I was just fuckin' with you," he said, narrowing his eyes at her.

"Shit, ain't no fun if your homies can't have none," Fast Blacc announced, raising up from the floorboard.

Lil Branon was startled, he almost side swiped the car in the next lane. The driver of the car blew her horn accelerating away. Lil' Branon turned around to see what his brain already knew.

"You need to watch the road pimp. And keep both hands on the mutha fuckin' wheel," Fast Blacc told him, letting the presence of the .380 be known, pressing it against the back of Lil' Brandon's neck.

"You should've stayed back home in Killeen and left this shit to us big boys. Damn Renee, puff puff pass bitch!" Fast Blacc said, reaching for the blunt with his right hand.

That was all the distraction Lil' Branon needed. He stomped down on the gas pedal making a hard-left turn slamming into a parked car. Fast Blacc and Renee flew to the right side of the car. Lil' Branon wasted no time jumping out of the car running at full speed. He was fast, but not faster than the bullets vomiting out of the .380 Glock. Two slugs plunged into Lil' Brandon's back causing his to fall face first into the concrete. Renee was screaming like she was the one who just got shot. Fast Blacc hopped back into the car burning rubber recklessly, with no thoughts for his own safety.

He didn't give a damn about nothing but putting miles between him and Lil' Brandon's body. His eyes were darting back and forth in each mirror. Renee was sitting with her back stuck to the door gaping at Fast Blacc with a frightening look on her face.

"You didn't tell me you was gonna kill him," she said, struggling to remain calm.

"He didn't tell me he was gonna do the dumb shit he did, now did he?" Fast Blacc told her, hitting the 610-freeway ramp going eighty-miles an hour.

He increased the speed even more merging over to the far-left hand lane. The faster he pushed the car the harder it began shaking.

"Boy, you need to slow down before the laws pull us over!" Renee hollered, turning around in her seat to see if the police were behind them.

"Turn your bitch ass around and be still!" Fast Blacc yelled, with an evil look on his face.

"Nigga, you ain't gonna be talkin' to me like I'm one of your hoes. You got me fucked up!" Renee hollered-out.

Those were the last words that left her mouth, before Fast Blacc bang the butt of the .380 Glock against her soft temple. If it wasn't for the seatbelt holding her, Renee would've been laid across the front seat. Fast Blacc pushed her body up against the passenger's door. He slowed the car down to a reasonable speed exiting I-10 East heading to Kelly Court apartments. Against his better judgement, he detoured to Coke apartments to purchase himself another extract bottle filled with formaldehyde. He glanced over at Renee who was still in another world. Fast Blacc reached inside of her bra taking his money back, along with whatever else she had made that night.

"You won't be needing this where you're going," Fast Blacc said, peering in the rearview mirror laughing to himself.

(THEY SAY IT'S OK TO TALK TO YOURSELF. BUT WHEN YOU START ANSWERING YOURSELF, THAT'S WHEN YOU'RE CONSIDERED CRAZY.)

CHAPTER 24

"LOOKING FOR ANSWERS"
(FEDERAL ROAD)
HOUSTON, TEXAS

Redline and Hollywood were at home. Redline didn't tell Hollywood about his get together he had with Lil' Branon and Tron. He noticed her attitude was changing by the day, so he kept his comments to himself. Redline couldn't judge her for the way she was acting when he was the one to blame. Shaking the thought out of his head he continued eating the meal she cooked for him. Hollywood prepared another one of his favorite dishes. She hooked up a seafood gumbo, shrimps, crabs, oysters, sausage, chicken, the works. When she had a lot on her mind, she released her stress by cooking. And lately, she's been putting Martha Stewart to shame. Redline reached for the remote control turning on the television. Surfing through the channels he settled for the news. The news was reporting on a missing person.

"THIS IS BRANDY TILLMAN, REPORTING LIVE FOR THE CHANNEL TWO NEWS. WE ARE HERE IN TENNESSEE COLONY, TEXAS, LESS THAN FIVE MINUTES FROM THE TEXAS DEPARTMENT OF CRIMINAL JUSTICE, COFFIELD UNIT.

THE POLICE ARE INVESTIGATING AN ACCIDENT OF A VEHICLE THAT BELONGS TO A T.D.C.J OFFICER. THE

COFFIELD T.D.C.J OFFICER WHO'S VEHICLE WAS ABAN-
DONED BY KIM'S CORNER STORE. THE VEHICLE WAS
INVOLED IN A COLLISION OF SOME SORT. FOLLOW UP
REPORTS SHOW THIS WAS THE OFFICER'S FIRST DAY
BACK AT WORK FROM HER VACATION. THERE ARE NO
WITNESSES AT THE SCENE OF THE CRIME. SO, IF ANYONE
KNOWS THE WHEREABOUTS OF MISS AMBER STACKS,
PLEASE CALL THE POLICE DEPARTMENT AS SOON AS
POSSIBLE."

Redline dropped his spoon calling Hollywood into the living room.
"Hollywood! Hollywood!" He hollered out.

"Boy shut up, so I can hear what she's saying," Hollywood said,
walking out of the kitchen staring at the television set.

She couldn't believe what her own eyes were witnessing. "Say baby,
do you have that bitch number that Amber fucks with?" He asked.

"You think Lyric had something to do with that?" Hollywood told
him, with a perplexed look on her face.

"N'all, I just wanna find out if she knows about Amber yet. And if
she knows anything else about Fast Blacc," He told her, finishing the
last of his food.

Hollywood gave him Lyric's number. She felt Redline had something up his sleeves, and it was just a matter of time before she rolled
them up discovering the truth. Hollywood knew his secrets would be
hard to find. But the love for her brother Pee Wee had her searching
for the truth.

(EVEN A FOOL CAN LOOK SMART, ONLY IF HE
KEEPS QUIET.)

CHAPTER 25

"EMOTIONALLY DISTURBED"
(11162 BRAESFOREST DRIVE)
HOUSTON, TEXAS

Lyric glared at the wall after hearing the news about Amber from Redline. She wondered if Amber was just missing, as her mind was toying with the thoughts of her being dead. Fast Blacc being involved was the next thought to jump in her mind. Things were getting worse by the day.

"Fuck, I'm pregnant by this nigga. Redline's calling me asking about Amber like I had something to do with it. Who in the fuck does he think he is?" Lyric thought to herself, walking around her house.

She couldn't stop thinking about what happened to Amber. "All of a sudden Redline's calling me asking about Fast Blacc. He's supposed to be fuckin' Fast Blacc up for the shit he did to Hollywood. He ain't did shit since he's been out of prison. What type of nigga does Hollywood have?" Lyric wondered.

Her brain kept picturing Fast Blacc. She wished she would have never approached him. The argument Fast Blacc had over the phone was still fresh in her mind. Redline was asking questions about Amber and Fast Blacc as if he was Johnny Cochran. Lyric felt she should've kept her mouth shut, and none of this madness would have happened.

"I wonder if, that was Redline on the phone talking to Fast Blacc?" Lyric thought to herself.

The thought of Redline being the caller Fast Blacc was hollering at over the phone, never crossed her mind until now.

"Maybe that's why this nigga is calling me all of a sudden. He's trying to figure out if I know if it was him or not. Why would he have his own brother-n-law killed?" Lyric wondered, as thoughts continued to run through her mind.

She decided to get to the bottom of everything, or at least try. She dialed Amber's cell phone. The call went straight to the voicemail. Her mind was so confused over Amber, Lyric didn't care about anything else.

"Fast Blacc knows something—Redline is hiding something—and Hollywood is looking for answers," Lyric mumbled to herself, sitting down thinking of a way to get everyone together at the same time.

(THE TRUTH WILL BE FREELY SPOKEN BY MOUTH. IF NOT, IT WILL BE BY ACTIONS.)

CHAPTER 26

"PIECES TO THE PUZZLE"
(FEDERAL ROAD)
HOUSTON, TEXAS

"What did she say?" Hollywood asked, as her eyes were glinting with suspicion and frustration.

"She said I was the first one to tell her," Redline said, flopping down on the couch. "And the last time she talked to her was when she got off of work," he told her, raising his eyebrows.

"Do you think Fast Blacc had something to do with it?" Hollywood asked.

"Ain't no tellin' right now. But by the way the news is talkin' about it, shit don't seem right." Redline hated being on the defense when Hollywood was offensively driving the ball. He went for the interception.

"How did you and Amber find out about Flagg gettin' shot?"

"I thought I told you that already," Hollywood said, kind of annoyed with the question.

"If I would've known I wouldn't have asked. What's wrong with you? You acting like your catchin' an attitude cause I asked a question," Redline told her, leaning back on the sofa.

Hollywood inhaled a deep breath blowing it out between her lips.

"Baby, I'm sorry it's not you. It's just all this bullshit is fucking with my head. I'm ready to put all this shit behind us," Hollywood explained, sitting down on the couch next to him. "Lyric told Amber that she heard Fast Blacc talking to somebody on the phone. Then Amber called and told me what was up," Hollywood kicked off her high heels reclining back on the couch.

Redline turned up his nose making a face as if her feet stank.

"Boy don't play!" she snapped. Redline sneered jumping right back on a serious note.

"How do you think Fast Blacc found out Lyric gave him up?" Redline asked, glancing at her fresh pedicured toenails.

"The only person I can think of is that bitch Mona. Amber told me she was mad at the hospital when Lyric told her," Hollywood said, placing her feet in his lap laying back across the couch. Redline began massaging her feet.

"Who in the fuck is Mona?" he asked, hiding his confusion.

"Mona is the bitch we tied up in Lyric's basement. I caught the bitch wearing Pee Wee's chain that I bought for him. So, Amber knocked her ass out. Lyric tied the ho up. And I was trying to beat some answers out of the bitch," Hollywood told him, closing her eyes enjoying the foot massage.

"What happen after that?" Redline asked, noticing Hollywood was enjoying the pleasure he was working through his fingertips.

"The bitch didn't tell me where she got it from. That was when the answer came walking down the stairs holding a gun. Fast Blacc!" she said, arching her back.

"Do you know where to find Mona at?" he asked, looking at the expression she had on her face.

"Yeah, she won't be any help though," Hollywood said, with a strained expression on her face.

"Why not?"

"Because she's dead, Lyric killed her. That's how she got away from Fast Blacc in Killeen. That went down before I talked to you. Remember you gave me the directions to that warehouse?" Redline nodded his head and continued rubbing her feet. "The police found her and some dude dead. Me and Amber saw the dude laying across the floor, but we didn't see Mona," Hollywood said, yawning while stretching her body like a purring cat.

Redline remembered Tron telling him something about a girl that was found dead along with Bug. He tried to piece Mona into the puzzle, but he couldn't figure out where to place her. Things were getting out of hand and Redline sure didn't see this coming with Amber. He looked down at Hollywood, she had fallen asleep. Redline called Lyric back to do a little fishing, he had to find out what she really knew.

(THEY SAY THE MIND IS A TERRIBLE THING TO WASTE.
SO, WITH THE RIGHT AMOUNT OF PLANNING,
ANYTHING CAN BE ACCOMPLISHED.)

CHAPTER 27

"LET'S GET IT STARTED"
(11162 BRAESFOREST DRIVE)
HOUSTON, TEXAS

Lyric finally decided that the only way to solve her predicament, she had to be more gangster than the rest. Sitting around looking stupid wasn't going to get anything ironed out. She hated taking the step she was about to take. Lyric picked up her cell phone searching through her call log for Fast Blacc's number. Once his number displayed on the screen, she sat there gazing at it. Lyric couldn't explain why she saved his number after all that had happened. Amber gave her the scoop on Fast Blacc, but she didn't tell Lyric how she used to watch him play with his big black anaconda, until it threw up everywhere. Lyric took a deep breath before dialing the devil's number. The line rung six times before it stopped.

The voice operator answered, "This person had a voice mailbox that has not been set up yet. Thank you, bye bye." Lyric ended the call then tried again. She was greeted by the same operator.

"FUCK!" she hollered out, setting her cell phone down on the coffee table.

Her brain was wandering like a lost child. The phone number was the only way to get in contact with Fast Blacc, and he wasn't answering. Her phone began vibrating on top of the table. She jumped. Lyric observed her cell phone fluttering across the table. She grabbed her phone peering at the number which she instantly recognized.

"Lowery Mitchell!" Lyric said, answering the phone. "Who the fuck is this?" Fast Blacc responded, stunned by hearing his birth given name.

"This is Lyric! And don't worry about how I know your fuckin' name. I know a little more about you than you think. But fuck all that, me and you need to discuss something very important." Fast Blacc wiped his hand along his pants leg.

"Bitch, we ain't got shit to talk about ho," Fast Blacc told her, nervously thinking back to Amber Stacks.

"Bitch-ass-nigga! I'm pregnant by your ho ass. So, unless you wanna be tracked down for eighteen-years, Lowery, I need some abortion money," Lyric said, placing emphasis on certain words.

"How do I know you ain't trying to run game on a nigga?" he asked, clenching his fist in frustration.

"Well, do you wanna go to the doctor with me? If not, you need to shit out that bread, so you can help with this problem," Lyric said, already speculating his answer. "What's up baby daddy?" she said, sarcastically.

This was one problem Fast Blacc didn't want. "Bitch, where are you?" he asked.

"N'all baby, you're the bitch! We'll hook up tomorrow after I come from the doctor's office. Just have my bread ready. Eight hundred dollars. When you get my text, you'll know where to meet me at," Lyric explained, clearly.

"I don't know who the fuck—!" Lyric ended the call before he finished talking. Her life was in her own hands, and Lyric was going to try her best to stay alive.

(MISTAKES CAN BE VERY FATAL. EVERY MOVE MUST BE CONTEMPLATED WITH PRECISE CALCULATION, LIKE A SURGEON PERFORMING SURGERY.)

CHAPTER 28

"BLIND SIDED"
(FEDERAL ROAD)
HOUSTON, TEXAS

Redline absorbed information from Hollywood that he didn't know she knew. He wondered if she was withholding anything from him. He never second-guessed Hollywood before, but he knew her capabilities if push came to shove. He grasped his nickel plated .45 walking out of the back door. The way things were going for him, Redline would rather be caught by the police with a pistol, than crossing his enemy without one. He hopped into his CTS and drove around the corner parking in front of a park. Redline left the house in order to call Lyric without Hollywood trying to put two and two together.

Lyric answered on the second ring, "Hello."

"Hey Lyric, what's jumpin' on your end?" she recognized the voice immediately, thinking to herself what does he want now?

"Ain't too much on my end, just waiting and hoping Amber calls."

"I'm feelin' that. I hope she's alright," Redline said, rubbing a hand across his head unconsciously. "Say Lyric, ain't no use in me beatin' around the bush. I'm trying to find out what you heard Fast Blacc say about Flagg?" he asked, glancing at a car passing by.

"What do you mean?" Lyric told him, instantly realizing the reason he called.

"Hollywood told me you was with Fast Blacc, and you heard him talkin' over the phone about Flagg."

"Yeah I was with him. That happened a couple of days after we met," she said, grabbing the diamond pendant on her necklace sliding it back and forth.

"Did you hear him say who did it?" Redline asked, firing up a Black & Mild.

"When I first heard him, I thought somebody was in my house the way he was hollering. He was telling somebody how he got paid to do a hit, and it didn't matter who done it, as long as it got done," Lyric explained, struggling to remain calm.

She didn't know who Fast Blacc was actually talking to over the phone, but by the way Redline was grilling her she knew something wasn't right.

"Was Flagg the only one you heard him talkin' about?" he asked, with his eyes flickering around the park.

"No!"

Redline's heart began to hammer as he felt his pulse beating like a drum in his ears.

"He said, nigga it ain't like you can do something. Then he started yelling, fuck you and that pretty bitch you got."

"Can you remember anything else?" Redline asked, taking a drag from the Black & Mild.

Lyric took a deep breath. "Redline, I know you were the one Fast Blacc was talking to on the phone."

Redline was at loss for words as he ran his hand across his face. "What—did you say?'" he asked, with his voice breaking in guilt.

"Nigga don't play dumb. Fast Blacc just ran his fucking mouth a little bit too much. At first, I didn't know it was you," Lyric said, noticing the quietness over the line, which was a dead giveaway.

Redline held the cell phone in his hand not even attempting to challenge her accusations.

"I know Hollywood don't know you had her brother killed. You even got your own homeboy laying up in the hospital. All because, you paid a big—mouth—dummy," Lyric told him, gaining self-confidence with each word she spoke. "Now how much is this worth to you?" Lyric asked, like a bona fide boss.

Each word she said made Redline bite down on the tip of the Black & Mild in anger.

Killing Lyric bounced around in his mind. "Lyric, meet me tonight at Scores, I'll have fifty-thousand dollars for you. And I'll help you find Amber too," Redline quickly plea bargained.

"Sounds good to me. But, I'm much smarter than the average bear. I know if you had Hollywood's brother killed, you'll be quick to kill me."

"You got damn right bitch!" Redline thought to himself, wishing he knew where to find her, pronto. He took a hard pull from the Black & Mild, causing the inside of his car to glow bright red.

"I'll tell you where to meet me at tomorrow. And if you don't show up, I'll tell Hollywood and the laws what's up," Lyric said, with a fierce determination.

She knew she had to go all the way out. She didn't have any solid evidence, and everything she speculated was her own assumption. Lyric smiled at the thought. Her cleverness and guessing paid off. However, she didn't know what she was getting herself into.

"Just call me when you're ready, I'll have the money," Redline said, ending the call.

Redline replayed the whole conversation within his head. The more he thought about it, the madder he became with himself. He wanted to kick his own self in the ass for being so stupid and folding under pressure. Never in his life has he told on himself. Then to make matters worse, he was crafted by a female that didn't know the facts. Even though Redline didn't admit to the rap, just by him offering to pay the money made him look guilty.

(THEY SAY THE BEST WAY TO GET SOMETHING DONE RIGHT, YOU HAVE TO DO IT YOURSELF.)

CHAPTER 29

"I'M THE BOSS"
(11162 BRAESFOREST DRIVE)
HOUSTON, TEXAS

Lyric threw her cell phone on the sofa screaming at the top of her lungs. She knew the plot she was scheming could back-fire, but she had to take that chance.

"One day you're here baby, and the next day you're gone. The next day you're gone." She blew air between her lips thinking about her favorite UGK song by Pimp C (R.I.P.) and Bun B.

Visions of Amber snatched her thoughts like a child abusing mother. Amber's image began attacking her brain triggering an emotional rage. Lyric grabbed a crystal vase center piece off the kitchen table, throwing it across the room. The vase shattered against the wall upon contact. Crystal pieces flew everywhere. Lyric tornado-ed through her kitchen smashing plate after plate, like a maniac on a mission. Her hair was moving in one direction, while broken dishes were flying in the other. Her kitchen was tore up like an episode of Extreme Makeover.

There were pieces of glass and porcelain chunks all over the floor and countertops. Lyric sat amongst her own destruction, crying and wandering why? She questioned whether Amber was alive or not? Would her life ever get back on track? There were no guaranteed chances that she would make it through tomorrow. Her nerves began calming down as she peered around at her handiwork. Lyric shook her head thinking this might be her last night alive.

She reached inside one of the cabinets, grabbing one of the miniature bottles of alcohol her girlfriend Brittney collected. Lyric opened a bottle of Patron taking a big swallow. She went into the bathroom hoping a hot bubble bath would ease her mind. She ran her bath water undressing in front of the mirror. Dealing with a killer like Fast Blacc, along with Redline, the odds weren't in her favor. Lyric felt she needed to party like it was her last night on earth...alive. But what she really needed...was a gun.

Admiring her body once more in front of the mirror, she stepped into the bathtub. The sounds of Mary J Blige were playing from the radio sitting on the counter. Lyric wondered how Mary J had a song for almost every way she felt? Every song Mary J sang, sounded like she was there when the situation occurred.

"CAN YOU LOOK IN MY LIFE, AND SEE WHAT I SEE?"

Between Mary and the soothing hot bubble bath relaxing her muscles, Lyric was feeling better. Can't leave out the fact, of the Patron warming her up on the insides. Lyric dried off before rubbing lotion over her body. Managing her hair, the best way she could, she slid her body into a pair of snow-white see-through bra and garter set. Pouring her ass into a pair of red denims, Lyric eased her arms into the sleeves of a black tailored leather jacket. She guided a black leather belt around her waist. Lyric paid TV Johnny eight-thousand dollars to make her a custom-made belt buckle. The whole buckle was laced with diamonds. Her initial was in the middle like Lavern, a cursive L. Lyric pulled on her black knee-high leather Gucci boots, which matched her jacket. Spraying on perfume called Hot Spot, she smiled at her reflection heading towards the door. She silently recited Psalm 23 before opening the front door.

(IT'S BETTER TO BE A NOBODY AND HAVE SOMETHING, THEN PRETEND TO BE SOMEBODY AND HAVE NOTHING.)

CHAPTER 30

"THE BEST FOR LAST"
(EDGEBROOK & HWY 45)
HOUSTON, TEXAS

Tron checked every strip club on both sides of the freeway. It was the same story every club he went into. Each dancer he talked to said, "We haven't seen him in a while," or "Do you want a lap dance?"

He knew the whores were trying to get paid, so he didn't knock their hustle. Tron just wasn't going to be the one contributing. Before Redline went to prison, Tron put his money into a strip club called "The Ritz." It was located off highway 45 South and Edgebrook. His aunt operated the club while he enjoyed the fruits of non-labor. Besides conversating about the club with his aunt, and collecting his income, Tron hasn't been to the club in over a year. That was the reason he chose to save the best for last.

Tron made a lot of trips along the highways, saving close to seven-hundred-thousand dollars. His goal was to stack a million dollars then move out of state. Trying to stack a million dollars was a lot of hustler's ambition. Tron had the will power to save his money for a future investment, instead of making it rain in strip clubs for attention. Tron thought about if he would've never met the rest of the clique, he would have never been in this situation searching for Fast Blacc. Some things happen for reasons, and Tron was about to find out why.

He pulled into a Chevron gas station on the corner of Edgebrook and I-45. He walked inside to pay for gas and a pack of Black & Milds. Pumping his gas, he noticed a money green, convertible Thunder Bird pulling into the gas station. The car pulled up next to his and the driver got out. She wore tight red pants which were molded around her butt, making it look sweet and juicy. The female driver bent over, reaching for something out of her car.

Black leather, knee high boots, and a heart shaped ass was a wondering sight. "You must be trying to get somebody to pay for that gas," Tron said, picturing himself behind her putting in work.

Her mind was occupied with heavy thoughts, so she didn't hear Tron talking to her. And Tron wasn't the one to be ignored. The sexy brown complected female walked out of the gas station, and he was all over her. "Maybe if you loosen up those tight ass pants you might feel better," he said, moistening his lips.

"What?" she answered, with a frown on her face.

"You heard what I said. I was talking to your pretty ass, and you walked right by me like I was a scrub or something," Tron told her, letting his eyes scan the catch of the day.

"Oh, I'm sorry! My mind is on something else right now," she said, fondling her hair.

"I thought you smelled my breath." Tron told her, with a smirk on his face. That was when he saw her pretty smile.

"My bad, my name is Tron," he said, reaching out to shake her hand, noticing the softness upon contact.

"My name is Lyric."

"That's a sexy name for a dime piece like you," Tron said, confidently.

Lyric stepped towards the gas pumps to hide the flush that was showing on her face. Tron sensed she didn't want to be bothered, but he refused to be rejected.

"You think I can take you out and get to know you a little better?" Tron asked, locking his eyes on her, watching as she filled her car with gas.

"I'm already out unwinding now."

"Where are you headed to?" Tron asked, lusting at the sight of her full lips.

"I'm finna check out The Ritz!" Lyric told him, screwing the cap tightly on her gas tank. Tron began laughing.

"What's so funny?" Lyric asked, with a slight attitude placing her hands on her hips. The look on her face said the rest.

"Hold up Miss Feisty, I own The Ritz. I just found it funny meeting a woman that's headed to the club I own," Tron said, displaying the club's logo on his iPhone.

Lyric glanced down at his phone before looking back up at him. Tron peeped her juicy full lips again. Her thighs were begging for attention.

"Say Lyric follow me; I'm headed to the club now." Tron said, jumping back in his car without giving her a chance to protest.

Lyric smiled getting into her car. The club was located on the opposite side of the freeway, so she didn't have far to drive. Tron called the club informing the crew he was pulling up in five minutes. When they arrived, Tron flagged Lyric with his hand, signaling for her to remain behind him. The V.I.P. treatment was in full swing. Lyric and Tron were escorted through a special entrance as their cars were being valet parked.

"Everything's on me, so enjoy yourself and get loose," Tron said, popping the top on a bottle of Krug pouring her a drink.

Lyric took the drink tossing it back. "Do you think I can get something stronger?"

Tron laughed ordering a bottle of Herradura and Grey Goose. The balcony sat above the main dance floor, making the atmosphere live, like the women performing. Tron stepped out on the balcony viewing his investment. The sight of beautiful women was everywhere. It didn't matter at The Ritz, every nationality was welcome, and they were all flaunting their sexiness. There were four bars, two full bars and two smaller ones located on each floor. A small bar was upstairs surrounded by three 72"-inch flat screen televisions. Each screen viewed a different football game on game day.

There were seven private dance tables situated under a see-through dance floor. Dancers were able to slide down each pole into the private area. Only three people were allowed in each area at a time.

"I assume you weren't going to let me know you were on the premises," Tron smiled as soon as he heard her voice.

"You can't bullshit the bullshitter. You knew I was coming before I step foot on the property," Tron told her.

"What does that have to do with you letting me know you're here?" she asked.

"If it'll make things better, I'm sorry for not checking in momma," he said, lowering his head down as if a little child who was caught doing wrong.

Diane playfully pushed him upside his head. Lyric laughed enjoying the alcohol streaming through her system. Diane was Bug's mother, and one of Tron's favorite aunts. That's why he approached her with the proposition of running a gentlemen's club. And just like he thought, Diane seized the opportunity to have money.

"Excuse me, but I came here to have some fun. So, I'm going downstairs where the party is jumpin," Lyric said, with her mind on getting drunk, hoping to escape reality for the night.

(DROWNING YOUR PROBLEMS IN ALCOHOL FEELS GOOD, UNTIL YOU WAKE UP IN THE MORNING.)

CHAPTER 31

"ALL OF A SUDDEN"
(FEDERAL ROAD)
HOUSTON, TEXAS

Redline woke up the next morning with Lyric on his mind. "I gotta get rid of this bitch," he thought to himself.

Hollywood was sleeping when he got out of bed, so he decided to fix her breakfast. He wasn't a chef like Mr. Cook, but he had a few ideas to arouse the taste buds. He scrambled eggs and fried a whole package of turkey bacon. He knew Hollywood loved hash browns so preparing them was a must. Toasted bread, lightly buttered, with grape jelly along with hot butter grits. Redline thought about the lie he was going to tell Hollywood about the money he needed.

"So, you weren't gonna tell me?" Hollywood said, startling him from his daze.

"Tell you what?" he asked, turning around facing her.

"That you were in here cooking breakfast," she told him, stretching her arms above her head letting out a slight yawn.

"I shouldn't have to tell you. Big as your nose is, you smelled the food cooking before me," Redline said, smiling, flickering a glance in her direction.

Hollywood turned her nose up. "Boy, as soon as I smelled the turkey bacon, I jumped my ass up."

"I was gonna serve you in bed like a real queen."

"It's not too late," she told him, walking back towards the bedroom.

"Hollywood, girl don't play."

She turned around laughing. "Boy, you know I gotta get mine in," she said, as they both sit down at the table. Redline took a sip of ice cold, Tropicana orange juice and got right to the point.

"When you finish eating, I need for you to get me fifty thees out the safe," he said, with his head down narrowing his eyes at her.

Hollywood gazed blankly waiting to hear the reason he wanted the money.

"What do you need fifty-thousand dollars for, if you don't mind me asking?" Hollywood said, taking a bite of hash brown.

Redline continued eating like he didn't hear the question she asked. He knew what the conversation would lead to, and he didn't feel like arguing with her this morning.

"Oh, you're just gonna sit there and play deaf and dumb?" Hollywood asked, raising her voice.

The way Lyric had deceived him already, Hollywood wasn't doing nothing but adding fuel to the flame. He glanced up at Hollywood. She wore a look on her face like she wanted to slap the shit out of him. Hollywood stood up from the table and walk towards the bedroom. Redline couldn't think of a good lie fast enough before she was back with the money.

"Here's the money. Now can you tell me what the fuck is going on?" she asked, sitting back down nibbling on a piece of turkey bacon.

"It's nothing to worry about. Just a little bait money I need to catch a live rat with," he quickly lied.

"A live rat! A live rat don't mean shit! What are you gonna do with fifty-thousand dollars? At least you can tell me what's going on. I might know of another way to help. That way we can keep the money. Have you thought about that?" Hollywood asked, biting down on a piece of bacon chewing angrily.

"Look here baby, what I'm about to do is a done deal. I'll lace you up on everything when I get back," Redline told her, finishing the rest of his orange juice. He grabbed the money off the table stuffing it into his pockets.

"So, you're just gonna walk away from me? You don't feel like I deserve an answer? All of a sudden you're a square business gangsta now, huh?" Hollywood said, with a poisonous look. "Don't forget, you only did one gangsta thing since you been home. Do I need to refresh your memory, pimp-daddy!"

Hollywood was working her way under his skin. Redline turned and walk towards the front door. She was right on his ass scratching deeper. Redline spun around to slap her into next week. To his surprise, Hollywood ducked the blow before counterattacking with two quick punches to his stomach. Redline drop down to his knees trying to catch his breath. Hollywood took a step away from him. She stood with her legs apart, knees bent, both arms extended holding a .32 automatic aim straight at him.

"I told myself the next time you put your hands on me, I was gonna kill you. Consider this your final warning," she said, looking malevolently at him.

Redline had never been hit in the stomach with such force in his life. He tried to utter something, but the pain exploded to his brain making him ignore what he had to say. Hollywood walked back to the kitchen table and continue her breakfast. The food was cold. The same way she was feeling, cold hearted.

"Your ass ain't sat still since you been home. What the fuck are you doing? I'm done put my life in danger more than once for you." Redline lay on the floor regaining his flow of air. He heard everything Hollywood was saying.

"Down there in the penitentiary showing hoes like Amber your dick. You probably was fucking too, huh?" she said, venting. Redline regained his composure, walking out of the house feeling like a chump.

(IF YOU'RE NOT PREPARED FOR ANYTHING, YOU CAN ONLY BE PREPARED FOR FAILURE.)

CHAPTER 32

Fast Blacc remained hiding in Renee's apartment in Fifth Ward. He carried her inside like she was drunk the night he had hit her with the butt of his gun. Renee slept the day away. When she finally woke up, she realized where she was at and went straight to the bathroom. Looking at herself in the mirror Renee saw the damage that was done to her face. Quickly snatching a pair of scissors from a drawer, she tip-toed to the front room where Fast Blacc was watching an old ESG video, SWANG AND BANG. The way he lay back on the couch Renee thought he was sleeping.

Fast Blacc didn't notice Renee sneaking up behind him. "SON OF A BITCH!" she yelled out, driving the scissors deep into his chest.

"AAAAH!" Fast Blacc woke up screaming.

Sweat was pouring down his face and body. He jumped up and walk towards the bedroom to check on Renee. She was laying across the bed holding an ice pack against her face. The dream he had felt real, he began rubbing his chest. The dream was toying with his brain. He grabbed the extract bottle· to dunk himself a sherm. He removed the filter from the cigarette before he lit it. The formaldehyde took control of his mind like a flick of a light switch. His first thought was calling Lyric to let her know what was on his mind.

"That little bitch got me fucked up," Fast Blacc said, reaching for his cell phone dialing her digits. "Can't no hoe tell me what to do." He dialed her number twice, but there was no answer. Taking the last hit off the sherm he sent her a text.

"BITCH PK UP BD." (bitch pick up baby daddy).

He waited for a response which never came. Fast Blacc lit a Black & Mild as his phone vibrated in his hand. He glanced down at the number before answering.

"What the fuck do you want Line? Your bitch ain't figured you out yet?" Fast Blacc asked, sneering as smoke stray through the air.

"I really didn't wanna call yo counterfeit ass. I just felt you needed to know we have a problem, and-!" Fast Blacc cut him short before he finished talking.

"Nigga, we don't have a mutha fuckin' thing!"

"Stupid ass nigga! The bitch you fucked knows what's up. She knows I paid you to do the hit on Pee Wee, cause you ran your fuckin' mouth. Do you know a bitch named Lyric?" Redline told him, with his voice filled with malice.

Fast Blacc took another drag off the Black & Mild. "Look out Line. I just talked to the bitch yesterday, and she didn't say shit about that," he said, blowing smoke through his lips.

"Man Fast, you can't be a dummy for the rest of your life. The hoe called demanding money to keep her mouth shut, or she's going to the laws," Redline said, grasping his attention. "She said she wants the money tomorrow."

"Say Line, the little slut called and told me she was pregnant, and she wanted abortion money to get rid of the baby," Fast Blacc told him, inhaling the Black & Mild. "So, when she calls, I want you there when I get rid of the bitch. After that we can go our separate ways," Fast Blacc explained, exhaling smoke through his nostrils.

"Man, I ain't tryin' to do no more talkin'. Let's get this shit over with before somebody else finds out," Redline said, angrily.

"We gonna do it like this nigga!"

Redline was all ears as Fast Blacc laid the script out. "I already know where to meet the bitch at. So, I'll ride with you that way the hoe might think I didn't show up. While you and her are choppin' it up, I'll pop the bitch and keep the money," Fast Blacc said, with a smile on his face. "We leave, you drop me off, and that's a wrap." Fast Blacc was a little smarter than Redline thought he was.

"Like they say on Coffield, bet that! Just hit me up when you're ready to roll out," Redline told him.

"Bet that hustla!" Fast Blacc said, before ending the call.

They both did the same thing simultaneously after talking to one another. Each one of them took a pull from a Black & Mild.

Fast Blacc sat his phone down on the table thinking about what he was going to do with Renee. He peered back at her laying across the bed. Her shorts were battling for position in between her ass cheeks. The sight of her golden-brown ass made his blood rush to his dick. He removed all his clothes throwing them on the couch. He eased his way towards the bedroom quietly like a thief in the night. The closer he got to Renee's fat round ass the harder his dick became. Fast Blacc started stroking himself standing in the doorway watching her.

He tip-toed into the bathroom looking around. Once he found what he was searching for, he looked back and saw Renee had one leg drawn close to her body. He squirted lotion on his dick and began masturbating. He imagined himself riding her from behind with her shorts and panties pull to one side. He was lost in pleasure he began grunting out loud.

Renee move slightly lying flat on her stomach. The sight of her ass cheeks jiggling made him lose control. He ejaculated flushing his kids down the toilet. Fast Blacc snatched down the shower curtain. He folded the shower curtain in half wrapping each end around his hands. Jumping on her back he wrapped the shower curtain around her head with extreme force. Renee was taken by surprise. The only thing she did was struggle. The more she gasped for air the quicker her death came. Her kicks slowed right along with her struggling. Her fingers were desperately trying to tear away the thick plastic. Her kicking stopped.

Her scratching ceased. Fast Blacc held her down a couple more minutes to make sure she was dead. He unwrapped the shower curtain from around her head spreading it across the floor. He lay her body on top of it then roll her up like a Taco Bell burrito. He folded the ends before shoving her corpse underneath the bed.

Walking back to the front room he lowered the thermostat to its lowest temperature. Next, he grabbed the extract bottle filled with formaldehyde, baptizing another More cigarette. Once the flame touched the end of the sherm he drew a deep breath. All his problems were temporarily solved by the time he exhaled. Fast Blacc sat down on the couch as the temperature began dropping lower, and lower.

(IF AT FIRST YOU DON'T SUCCEED, TRY AND TRY AGAIN.)

CHAPTER 33

"LOSING FOCUS"
(THE RITZ)
HOUSTON, TEXAS

Tron was standing on the balcony glaring down at Lyric skillfully moving her body. He completely forgot the reason of his mission. Pussy was most men weakness...and Tron was one of them. Lyric moved her body seducing every watcher in the club. The alcohol flowed through her system as the music made her body move. Her knee-high boots and leather jacket had her looking like a biker. Lyric showcased her skills like a true rider, even Ciara would have been proud. Dancing between her thighs was the only thing Tron had on his mind.

"So, would you like to deal with them or not? That way when they call back, I'll be prepared on what to tell them," Diane explained. Tron didn't hear a word his aunt Diane said.

"Boy, you're just like your no-good ass daddy. I guess being a dog runs in the bloodline huh. Do you hear me talking to you boy?" she asked, shaking her head.

"Yeah Auntie, I just have a lot on my mind right now," Tron told her, rubbing a hand across his chin narrowing his eyes at Lyric.

"I know you have a lot on your mind, the way that girl has her ass stuffed in them denims." Tron began laughing. That was one of the reasons he loved his aunt so much, she kept it real without exaggerating. She also saw straight through his bullshit.

"So, you got me all figured out now?" Tron asked, turning around facing her while sipping his drink.

"No, I don't! If I was able to figure men out, I would've been rich a long time ago. Tron, I respect your judgement on everything you do. You're a great business partner," she said, brushing back a strand of hair from her face with her hand. "However, in order to succeed in life, you must set aside the time for business and the time for pleasure. The only way the two can mix, is if you're a pimp. Then sometimes a pimp will get caught up in his feelings too," Diane said, as she gave him a hug. She kissed him on the cheek before walking off.

"I love you Auntie!"

"I love you too boy!"

Tron felt his aunt, but his mind was feeling Lyric more. The way she was working her ass it was calling his name. He poured himself another shot of Herradura, downed it, then walked downstairs.

"A time for business and a time for pleasure," Tron said to himself, walking down the stairs making eye contact with Lyric. "I hope it's a time for pleasure," he said, making his way towards Lyric who was dancing in her own world.

"I thought you were gonna stand up there and watch me all night," Lyric told him, wrapping both arms around his neck grinding against him.

"I was, but all this ass was calling my name," Tron smiled, caressing her butt. "And by me being the playa I am, I couldn't keep it waiting any longer," he told her, moistening his lips.

Lyric turned around backing her ass against his hardness.

"I didn't know they allowed guns in the club," Lyric said, smiling to herself grinding harder against him.

"You never know when a woman might need some help." They both laughed flirting heavily throughout the night.

Lyric tried her best drinking her problems away. The more alcohol she consumed, the wetter her pussy became. Her mind was stuck on the hard object Tron had concealed within his pants. One of the dancers made her way towards the table and began working her money maker in front of Tron. Her name was Naliah, and Tron knew her quite well. Naliah stood 5'8", she was twenty six years old, light brown complected with long pretty black hair. Naliah was a mix of Mexican and black and had a nice set of full lips. Her look was innocent and seductive. Her eyes were enticing.

Lyric gazed as Naliah grinded her ass in Tron's lap. Lyric envied the way Naliah was working her backside with finesse, feeling his hard dick. The sight of Tron and Naliah made Lyric hornier by the second. She stood up and kissed Naliah softly on her lips. Tron immediately took the party upstairs to the V.I.P. room before things got out of control. Peeping from behind the mirror tinted back drop of the three hundred-gallon, wall fish tank, Diane peer at Tron escorting two ladies upstairs to the V.I.P. room. She shook her head side to side sitting behind her desk. Diane loved her nephew, and she couldn't do nothing but laugh to herself. "Like father like son," she said to herself, unconsciously biting down on an ink pen.

Lyric didn't notice when she dropped her cell phone. Her and Naliah were entertaining each other. Tron reach down picking it up, noticing she had an incoming call. Assuming Lyric didn't hear her phone because of the loud music, he glanced down at the screen. "What the fuck!" he said to himself, glancing up to see if Lyric was watching him.

The number hooked his attention with the quickness, it was a number he knew. Instantly, his mind jumped back on track to his mission. Wondering how Lyric knew Fast Blacc came to his mind first. Could she lead him to Fast Blacc? Would she help him? Tron was close. He had a personal vendetta to settle with Fast Blacc. And if Lyric was one of his females, he would use her to get to him.

Lyric poured herself a glass of Herradura, throwing it down her throat. That was all it took; everything became a blur. Her mind started thinking about Amber. She quickly reached for her cell phone. A rush of panic filled her body when she didn't feel it. Lyric grimly looked at Tron walking into the room.

"Hey Lyric, you dropped your phone," Tron said, handing her the phone back.

Lyric focused her eyes on the screen. (1 MISSED CALL) Checking the miss call she prayed it was Amber. She stood gaping at the number without blinking. Her hands started shaking. That was when Tron said something.

"Say, are you alright?" You're staring at that phone like you're scared of something," Tron told her, out of suspicion.

"I gotta get out of here," Lyric told him, walking towards the stairs in a hurry.

The alcohol took control of her body making her stumble down to the floor. Naliah snickered when Lyric fell to the floor. Tron glanced up at her shaking his head. The way things were shifting quickly, Naliah knew the party was over.

"I'll catch you another time Tron. When you're not busy and when you're alone," Naliah said, walking downstairs. Her ass cheeks talked smack as she strutted her way out the room.

"I can't let you leave like this. You can barely walk, so I know you can't drive," Tron said, blocking her path. "Plus, the laws are everywhere, and I can't let you leave my place of business drunk. If something happens to you, I'll be the first one held responsible. I'll take you home, or you can call a cab, but you're not driving away from here," Tron told her, sternly.

"I got something important I need to do in the morning, and I can't be waiting for no damn cab," Lyric snapped, not wanting to hear anything he was saying.

"Check this out! How about we get a suite, and in the morning, I'll bring you back to your car. I feel like I owe you at least that."

Lyric thought to herself. It sounded like a good idea, especially since she didn't know where Fast Blacc was at. Lyric wondered why Fast Blacc was calling her.

"Do you have a real gun?" she asked.

"I see you like talking about guns, huh?" Tron said, laughing. "Yeah, I got one. You scared of your boyfriend?" Lyric looked up at Tron. "N'all, a baby daddy."

Tron has known Fast Blacc for a year, and he couldn't picture him having kids running around. He held Lyric tightly to keep her from falling. Tron smiled at the thought of Fast Blacc being a father.

"Everybody has secrets," Tron muttered under his breath. "Everybody has secrets."

(A BUSINESS CAN LAST FOREVER IF THE PROPER STEPS
ARE TAKEN. HOWEVER, PLEASURE CAN DESTROY
EVERYTHING IN A MATTER OF SECONDS.)

CHAPTER 34

"MORNING AFTER"
(FEDERAL ROAD)
HOUSTON, TEXAS

HOLLYWOOD...(5:25am) After a night of tossing and turning thinking about Redline, she decided to get out of bed. She sat on the bed looking at herself in the mirror of her solid oak dresser. "I wonder where do we go from here?"

Hollywood thought how their problems have made them become enemies instead of lovers. Redline had been with her majority of her life, from childhood to an adult. Living life without him was something she couldn't imagine. Hollywood knew when a man didn't come home at night, he was either in jail or with another woman. If he wasn't in jail or in another woman's bed, he was either dead or in trouble. The more she thought about her situation the more worried she became. Love is uncontrollable and can't be explained.

Hollywood close her eyes only to feel the tears cascade down her cheeks. Unconsciously, she cried mumbling a prayer under her breath. Her brain worked overtime playing tricks on her conscience. Her heart was turning colder each day she planned her wrath of vindictiveness.

"I guess I'll stop by and check up on Flagg. But first, I have to call my baby," Hollywood thought to herself, staring at her reflection in the mirror with a blank expression.

(A FOOL'S LIPS WILL MAKE ENEMIES; AND HIS MOUTH
WILL GET HIM KILLED.)

CHAPTER 35

"BACK ON NOTE"
(SUPER 8 MOTEL/AIRPORT BLVD)
HOUSTON, TEXAS

TRON...(5:27am) Gazing at Lyric laying across the bed sleeping. Thoughts began attacking his brain.

"All I have to do is keep an eye on this bitch and wait until she leads me to Fast Blacc's ho ass. If she really is his BM, (baby momma) he'll show up for sure. I wonder why she was staring at her phone like that? It don't matter—as long as I stay on top of my game—I'll find the nigga," Tron thought to himself, dialing Lil' Brandon's number again.

He couldn't figure out why Lil' Branon wasn't answering his phone. A smile inch across his face, as he pictured Lil' Brandon laying up having sex with Renee. Tron sent Lil' Brandon a text, (BEAT IT UP 4 ME).

Tron looked at Lyric with his fury hiding beneath the surface. "I need to wake this bitch up like an old school pimp," he thought to himself, standing over Lyric. He chose the smarter approach, and patiently waited.

(BEWARE OF A HEART THAT PLOTS WICKED THOUGHTS,
AND FEET THAT ARE QUICK TO RUN TO MISCHIEF.)

CHAPTER 36

"SHERM TIME"
(KELLY COURT APARTMENTS)
HOUSTON, TEXAS

FAST BLACC...(5:28am) "Damn, I wanted to get up at five," he said, hissing at his plan on getting up early to scoop up another throw away gat (GUN). He was moving fast, there wasn't any time for procrastinating. Fast Blacc quickly started putting on his clothes. While grabbing his shoes and hat, his eyes were level with the extract bottle filled with formaldehyde sitting on the table. Sneering. "It's always time to ease the mind," he thought to himself.

Fast Blacc flipped a cigarette into the clear substance watching as it absorb the liquid. He inhaled the strong fumes rising to his senses. He slowly touched the flame from the cigarette lighter to the tip of the sherm. (POOF!) The end of the sherm began flaming like an Olympic game torch before he blew it out.

The windows of the apartment were covered with a light coat of frost from the temperature being low. Fast Blacc inhaled the sherm slowly, and as deeply as he could. Holding his breath, his ears began ringing before the sound changed into a humming from afar. Exhaling, the smoke hung suspended in the air once it settled. His next hit was quick and hard, then he flushed the cigarette butt down the toilet.

Fast Blacc begin peering around the apartment for any clues that could lead back to him. Under his normal mind frame, he would have taken safer precautions. But, once the mind is clouded with a controlled substance, carelessness is the norm. "NO MISTAKES NO MERCY NIGGA!" Fast Blacc said, walking out of the door.

Redline didn't know about his original plan, which was to kill Lyric. And while Redline was thinking everything was over and done with, he was going to kill him too. Fast Blacc glanced around discreetly adjusting his gun in the waistband of his pants.

(STAY AWAY FROM A FOOL, BECAUSE YOU WILL NEVER HEAR ANYTHING SMART COMING OUT OF HIS MOUTH.)

CHAPTER 37

"HIDING OUT"
(THE GOLDEN MOTEL)
HOUSTON, TEXAS

Unaware of the danger lurking close by, Redline made a left turn into his old honeycomb hideout. It's been over eight years since his last visit. He parked his car in his usual parking spot. Looking around Redline notice. everything was still the same way.

"Some things never change," he thought to himself, peering through his rearview mirror. Redline notice Reno's car in the same place too. He also knew he was under surveillance by Reno, or someone in his family. Stepping out of his car, Redline walked towards the office.

Reno wore a big cheesy grin on his face watching Redline walk up. "Come in through the back," Reno mouthed, from behind the two-inch bulletproof glass that separated them.

Redline smiled when he saw Reno. Reno was one of the very few people that stayed loyal while he was down serving time.

"I don't know why I didn't fuck with Reno from the jump. I probably wouldn't been going through this bullshit," Redline thought to himself, walking through the back door.

"Redline, what's up my man? How long have you been out?" Reno asked, showing his friend love with a firm handshake.

"I just got out."

"And you made a special trip to your honeycomb hideout just to see me?" Reno said. They both began laughing.

"N'all Reno, it's a long story. I'll tell you about it another time."

"My man, you owe me no explanations. I'm the one who owes you," Reno said.

Redline went to prison with Reno in debt a hundred-thousand dollars, for four books (KILOS) he fronted him.

"Reno, I ain't doing no trippin' on nothin' that was left behind. My people ain't sweatin' it, so why should I?" Redline told him, raising his eyebrows.

"I understand where you're coming from my friend. But me and my people, we have morals. Our word is loyal. My family raised us under loyalty. If it was said, it will be done," Reno explained, walking back into his office.

"Say Reno, is my room still the same?"

"My friend, you know our hideout—I mean, your hideout is still there!" Reno hollered out from his office. "All the fish died, but I bought some more," Reno said, walking back into the room holding a Nike shoe box. "Here you go." Reno said sternly, handing him the shoe box.

Redline opened the box quickly scanning ten neat stacks of hundreds. "Reno!" Redline said, looking up as Reno began waving his hands while shaking his head no. Reno wasn't trying to hear anything about not paying his debt.

"I just wanted to say thanks. I also need a favor," Redline told him.

"Anything my friend," Reno said attentively.

"I want you to keep this money for me, until I'm able to come back and get it," Redline told him, before handing him the shoe box back.

"Well, it's here whenever you're ready for it," Reno said, taking the money walking back into his office.

"Say Reno, I need to kick back for a minute or two," Redline said, glancing around the room.

"Get the card, you know where it's at!" Reno hollered out from his office. Redline snatched the card up walking to his honeycomb hideout.

There were only a couple of hours before daybreak and Redline needed them to settle down. The motel room was the same way he left it eight years ago. He sat the .45 automatic on the bed and began wrestling with the fifty-thousand dollars that was stuffed in his pockets. As soon as he lay across the bed, he started thinking about the squabble he had with Hollywood.

(LOVE IS HARD TO UNDERSTAND AT TIMES, SO DON'T PUZZLE YOUR BRAIN TRYING TO FIGURE IT OUT.)

CHAPTER 38

"HOOD NIGGAS"
(DIXIE GAME ROOM)
HOUSTON, TEXAS

Three thugs were standing in the parking lot of the Dixie game room, selling dope and getting high like always in the hood. Across the street sat a hole in the wall motel called The Golden. That was were Bullet, J Man, and Bo went with their dope fiend whores.

"Man, that's a clean ass CTS," Bo said, as the white Cadillac turned into the motel.

"Who in the fuck is that?" Bullet said, staring across the street at the dude walking towards the office.

"Nigga look like a fake ass Al B Sure to me," Bo said, making them laugh.

"Check this out on some real shit. That nigga has his pockets on swoll right about now. And before one of you niggas ask me how I know? Just trust me on this one," J Man told them, passing the cherry blunt to Bullet without taking his eyes off of the motel. "That's how my pockets used to look before I fell off. Then the nigga rollin' factory behind tinted windows, tryin' to be low key. Do you niggas wanna get this easy money?" J Man said, licking his lips.

"Look out J I'm all in. I'm like Nate Dogg, I want it all. I can't speak for Bullet though," Bo said, waiting for Bullet to snap back.

"Nigga, if I was deaf, dumb, and blind, I wouldn't want your ho ass speakin' for me. I can always use some extra cash," Bullet said, blowing the long cherry stem off the end of the blunt.

"Say Bo, ain't you and that Arab mutha fucka cool?" J Man asked, setting the plan into motion.

"Yeah we alright," Bo told him.

"Don't look back when I tell y'all this, but the laws are makin' the block," J Man said, taking a hit off the Black & Mild biting down on the tip.

Bullet was the first dummy to look back. As soon as he did, the brake lights on the police car lit up like Christmas. That was all Bullet needed to see. He quickly darted across the street on the side of the motel. By the time the police turned around and hit the corner, Bullet pulled a David Blain on their ass. Bo and J Man both knew the police had no chance in hell catching Bullet. He was a trail-running, fence-hopping, back street-riding king. Bullet was the only person they've known, who knew almost every back-street route on the south side of Houston.

"I told the dumbass nigga not to look back," J Man said, shaking his head.

"Maybe you should've said look back," Bo told him, laughing. "Say Bo, go and holla at your boy and see what's up with Al B Sure," J Man said, taking another drag from the Black & Mild embracing his thought of getting paid.

Bo jogged across the street to see what was up. J Man sat inside of his car backed up in the Game room's parking lot facing the motel. He reached behind the passenger seat grabbing his gun from the floor-board. It was an old school long nose .357. J Man sat patiently in the car waiting for Bo to return with some good news.

Reno was putting the money back into his safe when the door chimed, indicating someone was entering the front door. He thought it was Redline coming back until he glanced at the monitors. "Look what the wind blew in," Reno said to himself, closing the safe.

Reno walk to the front to see what Bo wanted. He knew the young hustler from renting rooms to sleep with the dope fiend whores that ran around like roaches. "How's it going Bo?"

"Same shit, different smell nigga. What's up?" Bo asked. peering back at the Cadillac park in the corner of the parking lot.

"How can I help you out Bo? Are you trying to rent a room?" Reno asked with a funny vibe touching his senses.

"Do you know that nigga who just pulled up, driving that CTS?" Bo told him, pointing to the white Cadillac.

"No, I don't know him. Would you like for me to ring his room, and let him know you're here?" Reno asked, with a smirk on his face reaching for the phone.

Bo spun around so fast the necklace around his neck swung in the air. "No, no. I'm good. That's alright!" Bo said with his voice breaking from guilt Reno place the phone back down. "What room did he go into?" Bo asked, flashing a roll of money.

"Now come on Bo, you know I can't do that. How many times do we have to go through the same thing over again?" Reno said.

Bo mugged Reno with a look that said it all. "Yeah, Yeah. I know. Well I'll fuck with you later Hibib." Bo told him, walking out of the front office. Reno peeped Bo getting into a vehicle that was facing the front of the motel. Before getting Redline paranoid over nothing. Reno kept his eyes on the vehicle and its occupants.

(DON'T FAIL BEFORE YOU SUCCEED. ALWAYS BE AWARE OF YOUR SURROUNDINGS, CAMERAS ARE EVERYWHERE.)

$$$

While waiting. J Man got another cherry blunt with his fingernail dumping the tobacco outside of his car. He twisted up the blunt in a perfect roll. He fired up the blunt without glancing away from the motel. It had been three months since J Man went bankrupt, but it felt much longer.

"About time." he said to himself, watching Bo walk across the street with a scorn look on his face.

He flicked the headlights catching Bo's attention. "Man, that fool said he didn't know who the nigga was," Bo informed closing the car door smelling the good weed. "Pass that shit nigga."

"Did you find what room the nigga was in?" J Man asked, passing the blunt.

"No!" Bo told him, inhaling on the blunt with his vacuum lungs.

"We can kick down doors or wait until the nigga comes out. It don't make do difference to me.'" J Man said, gripping the .357 revolver hitting the blunt.

"I think he's in that corner room by his car," Bo said, stepping out of the car disappearing behind the back of the Game room building.

J Man sat pondering on what Bo had told him. Bo hopped back into the car sitting his .9mm on his lap. "We can make something happen now or wait until they change shifts in the morning. It's up to you. They switch out in a few hours anyway," Bo told him, not caring whatever J Man's choice was.

"Let's wait until your boy switches out. That way, he'll be gone and can't say shit," J Man decided.

"That's cool," Bo said, reclining his seat back enjoying his high.

The only thing on J Man's mind was dead presidents. They both sat back entertained by their own thoughts, of how they were going to spend their share of the money.

(JEALOUSLY WILL MAKE A PERSON HATE. ENVY WILL MAKE A PERSON PLOT. GREED WILL DESTROY IT ALL IN SECONDS.)

CHAPTER 39

"MY BABY"
(THE GOLDEN MOTEL)
HOUSTON, TEXAS

REDLINE...(5:26am) The cherry tip of the cigarillo glow bright as he inhale deeply. He slowly exhaled emptying his smoke filled lungs. His brain involuntarily jumped to the first time he brought Hollywood to his hideout. It was the day they became one. Redline took another hit from the cigarillo filled with Purple Kush. His memory began jogging around with his thoughts.

"I wonder if Hollywood's asleep. I ought to call her ass. I know she's still mad," he thought to himself, reaching for his cell phone.

Redline knew it was hard to find a real woman that was loyal to the fullest. "The games niggas play. After today, I hope things get back on track. No more fussin' and fightin' only fuckin' and suckin'," Redline smiled at the thought, taking a hit of his medication.

His mind began churning, plotting and scheming, thinking about any loose ends leading back to him. Redline knew when a plan was thought out by a different person, it always sounded good. However, when he took the time out and did his homework, their mistakes became visible.

"Hell n'all!" He thought to himself. "I'm not rollin' in my ride. I gotta rent me a dope fiend rental through another fiend, just in case. Then I gotta kill both of their ass," he thought to himself, flushing the cigarillo down the toilet.

(5:35am) The screen on his cell phone lit up, the smile on his face did the same. He felt better knowing he wasn't the only one who couldn't sleep. "This has to be a gangsta bond," he thought to himself. answering his phone. "Hey baby!"

(LOVE HURTS, LOVE DOESN'T LOVE NOBODY. LOVE WILL KILL. LOVE SHOWS NO PREJUDICE.)

CHAPTER 40

"STAKE OUT"
(DIXIE GAME ROOM)
HOUSTON, TEXAS

J Man and Bo sat in the car for a couple of hours before making the block parking along the side of the motel. "When is your boy comin' up outta that bitch?" J Man asked, with greed rising in his throat.

"Nigga, that ain't my mutha fuckin' homeboy neither," Bo said, biting down on his teeth in anger. "Just chill nigga, he'll be rollin' up outta there in a few minutes. Just watch!"

"Man, I'm ready to get this shit over with and count that cash," J Man told him, touching the cigarette lighter against the tip of the Black and Mild coated with Big Moe (promethazine with codeine cough syrup).

They sat quietly waiting. Both were hungry and ready, each tasting the easy money. The guns in their possession had them experiencing the same feeling, POWER AND AUTHORITY! Reno checked the monitors several times before getting ready to leave. The vehicle never returned.

Reno called Redline informing him about the nightly events that took place. As he was driving out of the motel heading home, Reno glanced both ways, then turn right. If he would have only paid a little more attention, he would have seen the same vehicle from last night.

(EVERY MIND IS NOT CAPABLE OF HANDLING THE

STREETS: THOSE ARE THE ONES WHO USUALLY SUCCEED.)

$$$

J Man and Bo exchange glances with each other when they saw the black Acura drive away from the motel. "That's him!" Bo said, sitting up in his seat.

"Soon as he's outta sight, let's move," J Man told him, passing Bo half a blunt he just fired back up. They peer at the black Acura turning left at the end of the block.

Redline was talking on his cell phone with Hollywood when Reno called his room.

"That's the reason you wanted to leave, so you can get a room for your little bitches," Hollywood said, angrily.

"Girl shut up," Redline told her, answering the phone.

"Yeah what's up?"

"You had a visitor last night interested in your room number."

"Who was it?" Redline asked.

"I know of him, but I don't know him personally. He was trying to find out who you were," Reno said.

"What did you tell him?"

"I told him yeah, I knew you! And I let him know what room you were in," Reno told him, laughing at the stupid question.

"I tripped out huh?" Redline sneered, shaking his head.

"I watched him walk across the street and get inside a car. I'm getting ready to switch out now, so I was calling to let you know what's up. The car is not parked across the street anymore," Reno explained.

"Good lookin' out! I'm finna roll up outta here anyway."

"Call my cell if you need anything my friend," Reno said, before hanging up the phone.

"What was that all about?" Hollywood asked, as soon as Redline hung up the phone.

"Some nigga came to the office lookin' for me," Redline told her, placing his cell phone against his left ear.

"What are you gonna do?"

"I'm getting ready to leave alright. I love you," Redline said, ending the call. He grabbed the money off the bed stuffing it back into his pockets.

He palmed his nickel plated .45 before loading a bullet into the chamber. Redline carefully moved the curtain back peeking out of the window. He couldn't get a clear view because of the brick pillar blocking half of the window. He opened the door trying to get a better look at the entrance way. "FUCK!" Redline closed the door in a hurry.

"FUCK! FUCK! FUCK!" He saw a pistol in one of their hands. Instantly, he knew right away those were the thugs Reno told him about. "Think nigga, think." He looked around the room trying to maintain focus. Redline didn't know if they had seen him or not and running out there shooting like a fool wasn't an option. Glancing around the room again, he looked towards the bed. Redline quickly tried to crawl underneath the bed. That way, he would have a better advantage if they ran in shooting. He tried squeezing under the bed. That was when it moved.

"Let's roll out," J Man told Bo, when the black Acura turn the corner. J Man left the car running. They exited the vehicle with money on their minds. Bo kept his gun concealed from plain view walking into the parking lot. J Man frown up, nodding his head at a dope fiend whore he knew really well. No words were said between the two. J Man pointed at the Cadillac handing her a twenty-dollar bill.

"Twenty-five!" she mouthed, walking away.

J Man and Bo were the only two in the parking lot. Dawn was beginning to break as silver streaks of day light lit the sky. J Man point at the door signaling with his fingers, "Twenty-five." Bo nod his head up and down tightening his grip on his pistol. Room 25 sat in the corner of the motel. J Man peek around the corner making sure no one was hiding. Holding his gun tightly, J Man kick in the door. The door flew open with ease. Bo quickly ran towards the bathroom with his gun leading the way. Empty! J Man stood in the doorway puzzled. He turned around to leave. "Damn!" He said to himself, walking out of the door.

$$$

While trying to squeeze underneath the bed it began moving upwards. Redline push the bed up with his back raising it vertical. There was a mirror underneath the entire bed, displaying his astonish expression. Wasting no time, he jumped between the bed and the opening in the wall. "Man, this is some crazy ass shit," He said to himself, hiding inside a Murphy bed gripping his .45 automatic. A couple more minutes zip by. (BAAAM!). The door flew back with such force the 52" flat screen came crashing down to the floor.

"Check the restroom nigga," J Man said, raising his voice sweeping his gun across the room.

"Ain't nobody in there," Bo told him, with disbelief in his voice. They look around the room.

"Let's get out of here before the laws come," J Man said, walking out of the door.

"All these bitch ass mirrors, I know something is in this mutha fucka," Bo said to himself, peering at the fish tank. Once he saw the jewelry at the bottom of the fish tank, a smile spread slowly across his face.

J Man walk back to the door. "Man, bring your stupid ass on before the laws come.

"But they got a bunch of—!"

J Man walk off before Bo finish talking. "That's why I don't fuck with niggas now," J Man said to himself.

"This nigga on some girl shit," Bo mumbled, stuffing jewelry in his pocket walking towards the door.

"AAAHH!" Redline yelled out, pushing the Murphy bed down on top of Bo's head. (BOOM, BOOM, BOOM!) Redline shot through the mattress running to the door just in time to see J Man going down the entrance way. Redline squeeze off a couple more shots. (BOOM, BOOM!) None of his shots hit their target.

(BOOM BOOM!) Chunks of concrete flew in Redline's face before he dove to the ground. From underneath the car he was hiding behind, he saw a pair of feet running. Redline got up running to his car. He almost tore up his CTS trying to get out of the parking lot so fast. J Man was reversing down the street side swiping cars along the way. (BOOM BOOM!)

Redline let his pistol throw up a couple more bullets into the front windshield before driving away. Redline peered grimly in his rearview mirror making a few left and right turns. Feeling comfortable that he was no longer in danger, Redline eased his foot off of the gas pedal. He tried to figure who was out to get him, and why? Was it his past catching up with him after all these years?

(ANYONE CAN BECOME A VICTIM AT ANY GIVEN MOMENT. THERE ARE NO RULES IN THE STREETS.)

CHAPTER 41

"NO WAY OUT"
(SUPER 8 MOTEL)
HOUSTON, TEXAS

LYRIC...(5:30am) She lay across the bed as Tron peeled her red denims down, exposing her precious fruit. He slowly kissed her feet while making his way to the back of her knees. Tron placed two fingers inside of her wetness spreading her ass. Not being the type that lays around, Lyric raised her ass up in the air for easier access. Tron lower his head, tongue out ready for action.

"Ooooh!" Lyric moaned out, before opening her eyes. She quickly felt her body determining her clothes were still on. Lyric tried remembering what all had happened, but her mind wouldn't allow it. Her only memory was Tron and Naliah at the club. Lyric sat up looking at her surroundings. Her eyes quickly scanned the room, noticing her car keys and a piece of paper on the table. She got up and walk into the bathroom.

She looked at herself in the mirror forcing a smile. She knew she couldn't follow through with her plan feeling the way she was. She turned the sink on splashing cold water on her face. Lyric completely forgot about her cell phone, until it began vibrating in her jacket pocket.

"What the fuck do you want?" Lyric barked, thinking the caller was Fast Blacc.

"I want your sexy ass to come down here and pick me up from this airport. If you're going through things, I'm pretty sure I can get someone else to come down here," Brittney said, nonchalantly.

"Baby I'm sorry, I've been through a lot since you left," Lyric said, walking out of the restroom.

"Is everything ok?" Brittney asked.

"Yeah, I'll lace you up. I'm on my way now," Lyric told her, ending the call. She forgot she was supposed to pick Brittney up from the airport today. Lyric picked up the note Tron left on the table reading it.

"DIDN'T WANT TO WAKE YOU UP, YOUR CAR IS IN THE PARKING LOT. CALL ME WHEN YOU GET A CHANCE. (713) 991-2522 TRON."

Lyric put the note in her jacket pocket, snatched her car keys off the table heading out the door. Her car was parked right in front of the room. She deactivated her alarm and got inside. She selected her Sade's Greatest Hits CD, placing it into the Pioneer CD deck before rolling out. She lowered the convertible top speeding down Airport Blvd. The morning air rushed against her face blowing through her hair. Lyric thought how quickly a month flew by while Brittney was gone, and how fast she fell in love with Amber.

Tears zipped along the sides of her face as she ran through a red light, thinking about how fast her life was changing. She didn't want Brittney involved in her madness, but she needed someone to talk to. She removed her shades so the wind could dry up her tears before reaching Brittney. She took a deep breath turning into the airport. Lyric exhaled when she saw Brittney standing there looking like the professional, model/actor she was aspiring to become.

Brittney stood 5'2", pretty redbone, with doe-shaped eyes. Her hair was naturally curly hanging past her shoulders. Her facial features had a slight look of Native American. Brittney stood there with one of her hands on her hip, and the other holding onto her roll away luggage. She had on a pair of black Jam Mings, with a stylish leopard print skirt, black camisole underneath a white blazer. She smiled when she saw Lyric pulling up. Brittney threw her luggage in the backseat hopping into the car. They shared a passionate kiss. Several onlookers were pointing and gaping.

"I was about to ask you did you miss me," Brittney said, reaching for her seatbelt as Lyric drove away.

"Since you didn't ask, I don't have to tell you then," Lyric smiled, peering in her side mirrors changing lanes to enter the freeway.

"Oh, somebody became a little feisty since momma's been gone," Brittney told her, licking her lips eyeing Lyric. "Don't worry! I'll spank that ass when we get home, maybe your attitude will change then," Brittney smirked, relaxing back in the passenger seat.

"I think I'm too big for whippins momma," Lyric told her, merging onto the freeway.

"We'll see!" Brittney said, closing her eyes.

Lyric's thoughts jumped to Fast Blacc, thinking he was the person calling her this morning. The call from him or Redline would come soon or later. The ball was in her hands. She had something both wanted...her life! Lyric glanced at Brittney smiling at the sight of her hair blowing everywhere. She thought about Ice...her first boyfriend...and the main reason for her crossing over to women.

Ten years ago. Lyric was at a graduation party her homegirls put together for her at Club T Town. Ice was there with a couple of his homeboys. They all went to Milby High School together. Lyric walked to the bar for her second, Long Island Iced tea. Ice had his gaze locked on Lyric since she first walked into the club. She was the only reason he came to the club in the first place, and his homeboys knew it too.

Ice and Lyric had gym class together which was his favorite period. He would sit in the bleachers and watch Lyric as she exercised, played volleyball and basketball. Ice loved the way her shorts would make their way between her ass cheeks, exposing her fat rump. Every time Lyric pulled her shorts out of her butt, she would catch Ice looking. He would always shake his head or lick his lips. Whenever they made eye contact, his whole face would blush. They played games with each other for over a month, until Ice finally built up his nerve to approach her and introduce himself. They were on a hi and bye relationship until the day of her graduation.

"Look out guey! (homeboy) How long are you gonna stalk that black pussy before you ask for some?" Lucky asked, passing the eight-ball of cocaine underneath the table to Cho Che.

"You know that nigga scared of that nappy dug out," Cho Che said, peeping around to see if anyone was watching before taking a hit of Tony Montana (cocaine).

"Both of you niggas got me bent. Just cause I ain't never fucked a black hoe before, that don't mean shit," Ice told them, walking off towards the bar. Ice didn't know why he was shy when it came down to approaching black girls. He knew Cho Che and Lucky were sexing them down on a regular basis.

"Say guey, that nigga is going after that pussy," Lucky said, taking another hit from the sack of powder. "I bet you that nigga strikes out. I got the next Eightball on it," Cho Che told him, staring at a young dime piece he was about to step to.

Lucky peered at his homeboy slicing through the crowd, as if he was a panther on the prowl seeking its mate. "Look out Homito, that's a bet!" Lucky said, with confidence in his boy Ice.

"Don't score none of that bullshit when you lose," Cho Che told him, taking another hit intensifying his high.

"It ain't to much of no bullshit, the way you're sucking it up your shop vac nose," Lucky said, laughing.

"You got down Mexican. I'm finna go snatch that Alica Keys lookin' bitch right there. I'll fuck wit cha later,'" Cho Che said, pointing her out before walking off.

Lucky snorted a couple more hits then walked to the dance floor. Lyric was standing by the bar wearing a pair of blue high stepper boots, with a pair of black leggings. The bright double-breasted blazer gave her a conservative sexy look. Ice had his eyes glued to her backside as he moved across the club. The closer he got to Lyric the fatter her ass came into view.

"Damn Lyric, your gonna make somebody go to jail with all that ass you got," Ice said, rubbing his hands together with a crooked grin on his face.

"Just make sure you're not the one going to jail," Lyric told him, recognizing his voice instantly. "Do you want something to drink?"

"N'all I'm cool. I came over here to see if you wanted something. Plus, I wanted to stop playing these high school games, and see what's up with you," Ice said, with determination.

Lyric didn't know if it was the Long Island Iced Teas talking to her, or if she heard Ice correctly. "What did you say?" she asked, turning around to face him.

"I wanna know do you have a Vato?" he told her.

"What's a Vato?" Lyric asked, taking a sip from her drink. "It's a man, or a boyfriend," Ice said, with no intentions of letting up before succeeding his mission.

"N'all, I don't have a Vato! Do you plan on being mines?" Lyric asked, bashfully batting her eyelids.

That was the day her life changed, and she remembered it like it was her birthday. Her and Ice moved into a three-bedroom house together a year after her graduation. That was when she really found out what Ice had his hands off into. Ice had relatives moving kilos of cocaine across the border faster than a NASCAR. So, he seized the opportunity and grabbed himself a high-level position in the game. Him and his homeboys had the southeast side of H-Town (HOUSTON) on lock.

The more money Ice made the more he became insecure with Lyric. He wasn't allowed back on Texas Southern University campus, because he broke a dude's jaw and collarbone for talking to Lyric. Lyric was conversating with a dude in her class as she noticed Ice driving up. Ice jumped out of his car then walked right up to him without saying a word. Ice started beating him silly. Lyric tried to stop his as he stomped the dude's face into the concrete. The campus police came and restrained Ice and took him to jail. That was his first time ever being in trouble with the law, he was given probation and a lightweight fine to pay.

Lyric thought back to the day her and Ice were picking up money from several of his associates. Ice pulled up to a house and parked on the side of the curb.

"Honk the horn if you see anybody coming down the street," Ice told her, before he stepped out of the car.

Lyric peered at him as he walked in front of the car right up to the front door and knocked. A big Fat Joe looking Mexican opened the door then glanced up and down the street. Him and Ice were having a heated conversation from the looks of it. The fat Mexican poked his finger in Ice's chest. Lyric stared on. In one swift motion Ice pulled out his gun and shot him in the face. Blood sprayed over the front door. Lyric was appalled as Ice walked up to the passenger side of the car.

"Scoot over and drive!" Ice told her, opening the car door.

Lyric obeyed like a good little bitch, with no questions asked. From that day forward she became Ice's designated driver when things needed to be handled. One-night Lyric was awakened from her sleep. Ice told her to get dressed and "LET'S GO!" This was her first time taking a trip with Ice this late at night. Ice directed Lyric all the way to Duecing Park on the northside of Houston. She drove to the back of the park by the boat ramps and docks that sat in Lake Houston. Lyric parked then turned off the car like she was instructed. Ice popped open the trunk before he stepped out of the car. He raised the trunk up, reached inside with both hands, and heaved a black plastic tarp over his shoulders. Lyric gaped around when she noticed what appeared to be a body inside of the black plastic tarp.

She followed Ice towards the boat that was waiting at the dock. Cho Che was the first person she saw standing on the dock. Lucky was spreading another plastic tarp across the deck of the boat. Cho Che reached down and grabbed the body from Ice, and drug it onto the boat.

Her and Ice stepped on the boat then Lucky eased off towards the middle of the lake. After a thirty-minute silent ride Lucky killed the motor. Cho Che cut the plastic open without any hesitation and cut the eyeballs out of the man's face. Lyric leaned over the side of the boat and threw up the last thing she ate into the water.

"I bet you his ass won't see shit to tell now," Cho Che said, stuffing one of the eyeballs into the man's mouth, and throwing the other one deep off into the lake.

"Damn wetback, you need to try out for the Astros," Lucky told him laughing, as he tied four, forty-five-pound free weights around the ankles of the body. Lucky then pulled out a knife and started stabbing the body over repeatedly. Ice kicked the weights overboard as Lucky shoved the body. When the body splashed into the water, they all laughed, except Lyric. Lyric was too scared to even attempt to leave Ice after that.

They say GOD works in mysterious ways. A few months later, Ice went to jail for killing an associate who thought he was slick. That was well over ten years ago, and Lyric hasn't seen Ice since. Life goes on, and Lyric had a chance to change her life for the best. She was glad she was one of the lucky ones to escape the madness of being with a homicidal drug dealer. Lyric glanced over at Brittney before exiting the freeway on Greens Road. She decided to put her plan on freeze until she was able to get herself back together. Her life was on the line and she didn't feel like checking out at a young age.

(THE STREETS WILL BITE YOU IN THE ASS AT ANY
SECOND, SO BE PREPARED.
YOU WILL REAP WHAT YOU SOW.)

CHAPTER 42

"ONE STEP AHEAD"
(DOWNTOWN AQUARIUM)
HOUSTON, TEXAS

Fast Blacc sat in the parking lot of the Downtown Aquarium restaurant in another dope fiend rental car. Instead of waiting for Lyric to call him he decided to be there before she showed up. He thought about her being pregnant with his child.

"Baby momma!" he said, with a smile sneaking across his face. "I like the sound of that." Even though his mind liked to play games, Fast Blacc knew Lyric had to die. He thought back to the murders he committed without remorse or respect for the law.

BUG...He was at the right place, but with the wrong person. His only mistake was befriending a maniac that didn't give a damn. Fast Blacc felt the only ones who deserve to live were the ones who knew absolutely nothing about his dilemma. Bug was a true homey indeed. He was down for whatever with no questions asked. But, Fast Blacc felt differently. "NO MISTAKES NO MERCY NIGGA!"

MISS STACKS...There were no explanations needed about why he ended her life. "She knew who I was - she knew my real name. She escaped death once. She just knew to fuckin' much," Fast Blacc thought to himself, thinking back to how Tiffany helped him restrain Miss Stacks. After restricting her movement with duct tape, Fast Blacc drugged Amber across a dirt road into the woods behind Eisenhower Park. It was there he smashed her face in like an aluminum can.

Amber gaped with fear in her eyes. She watched Fast Blacc Pick up a boulder from the edge of the water. Her eyes screamed, begged, pleaded and cried tears. Fast Blacc struggled closer with the boulder held high above his head. Amber started kicking and flopping around as if she were a fish out of water. Her eyes bulged with fear, screaming "Please, No," for the last time. His arms shook under the weight of the boulder.

"NO MERCY BITCH!" he said, as he dropped the boulder down on top of her face.

Amber's body shook uncontrollably before it subsided. Her body twitched involuntarily for a few seconds then it ceased. Blood covered the leaves and ground surrounding her smashed head. Fast Blacc rolled the boulder away with his foot and grimaced at the sight. He reached down and grabbed her by the ankles. He dragged her to the secluded, reptile infested, body of water then threw her in. He quickly picked up the boulder and threw it into the water too. If it wasn't for the wet (FORMALDEHYDE) intensifying his strength, there was no way he would have been able to accomplish such a violent murder without stopping to rest.

Fast Blacc looked at his watch wondering why Lyric hadn't called yet.

"I guess this bitch think it's a mutha fuckin' game," he thought to himself, glimpsing at his cell phone.

He dipped another cigarette into the vanilla extract bottle fill with formaldehyde. He looked as the tobacco quickly absorb the liquid like a plant in the desert. Fast Blacc lit the end of the sherm. (POOF!) He peered into the flame thinking.

TIFFANY...He knew Tiffany was the most loyal female he had on his team, and by killing her so soon he felt he made a mistake. He had a few more obstacles to hurdle, and the best way to tackle a problem is with some help. Fast Blacc exhaled the sherm smoke through his nostrils until his lungs were empty.

RENEE...She was the type of bitch that couldn't be trusted as far as she could be seen, more like himself. How could he trust a person that was playing two ends to the middle? Renee had her mind on her money, when her brain should have been on who she was dealing with.

"Ha Haaaa! NO MISTAKES NO MERCY BITCH!" Fast Blacc laughed out to himself.

His eyes scanned the parking lot. He was scoping for Lyric or any other threat. There were only a few cars in the parking lot, and most of them belong to the employees. He took another hit from the sherm filling his lungs to the max. He placed his car into drive and was about to pull away when his cell phone began vibrating in his lap. Fast Blacc reached down grimly sneering at the number.

"I was wondering when the fuck you was gonna hit me up," Fast Blacc answered, exhaling the smoke as his nostrils flare up.

(IT'S BETTER TO RUN THROUGH A LIONS DEN WITH PORKCHOP UNDERWEAR ON, THEN TO ASSOCIATE WITH A FOOL WITH DUMBASS IDEAS.)

CHAPTER 43

"SOMEBODY'S WATCHING ME"
(GREENSPOINT)
HOUSTON, TEXAS

Lyric thought her mind was playing tricks on her driving home from the airport. She could have sworn a black 745i BMW with tinted windows was following her. She shook the thought out of her head assuming her hangover had her hallucinating. Lyric pull into Brittney's apartments, noticing the same black BMW turn into the corner store parking lot. She told Brittney about most of the events that transpired while she was away.

That was when she revealed to her about the car that was following them. They brush the threat aside temporarily and passionately made up for the days they were apart. After a little sexual gratification and a few hours of sleep, Lyric was ready to make her move.

"Brittney are you ready?" Lyric asked, as they exchange glances.

"If you're ready I am," Brittney told her, swallowing her nervousness.

Lyric smiled at Brittney. She knew Brittney wasn't accustomed to participating in any type of wrong doings. "If she only knew!" Lyric thought to herself. They got into the car.

"Brittney all you gotta do is lay your seat all the way back and chill," Lyric told her, checking her .32 chrome automatic.

Brittney had an appalled look on her face gaping at the gun Lyric was holding in her hand.

"W What—are you going to do with that?" Brittney asked, sounding as if she had a speech impediment.

"I hope nothing, but it's better to be safe than sorry," Lyric told her, hiding the gun in her sweat suit pocket. Lyric drove out of the apartment complex peeping at the black BMW park across the street.

"I knew I wasn't crazy," Lyric mumbled, biting her lip in frustration.

"What is it?" Brittney asked, nervously shaking like a pair of dice in a crap game.

"The car I was telling you about is at the car wash," Lyric said, peeping in her rearview mirror as the BMW stop at the end of the exit. She turned into the Citgo's parking lot on Greens Road, hopped out of her car and walk in the store. A few minutes later the green Thunderbird drove back to the apartments.

(INSTEAD OF SAYING, "I SHOULD HAVE FOLLOWED MY FIRST THOUGHT, JUST DO IT!)

$$$

Tron sat posted up behind the Citgo corner store on Greens Road at the car wash. The apartments Lyric drove into only had one-way in and one-way out. He sat with his car idling hiding behind the mirror tinted windows, preparing to get high. Tron reached for a loose razor blade gutting the chocolate blunt with one swipe. He opened his car door to dump out the loose tobacco. The wind blew it everywhere before it had a chance to touch the ground. Tron laced the inside of the blunt with a light coat of syrup (PROMETHAZINE & CODEINE) then fill it with pineapple kush. Twisting the blunt to perfection, he blazed it up.

Tron inhaled the good kush wondering why he hadn't heard from Lil' Branon. He knew it didn't take that long to get his dick wet. He tried calling Renee to see if she made it home. Tron was really calling to find out if Lil' Branon was over there. Her phone rang and rang, as a bad feeling started sneaking up from the pit of his stomach. Instead of taking heed to his subconscious, Tron brushed it aside.

The smoke floated on the inside of his car as if it was a morning fog. Tron peered across the street as a car exit the apartments. He thought about what Redline said about paying Fast Blacc to kill his brother-n-law. "That nigga has no remorse when it comes down to the game. He reminds me of somebody—I know real well," he thought to himself, inhaling the kush feeding his hungry lungs.

"I'm on you bitch!" Tron said to himself, adjusting his seat watching the green Thunderbird drive out of the apartments. He kept his distance to a minimum barely enough not to be seen.

He stopped when Lyric turned into the corner store's parking lot. Tron reversed his car a few feet to keep out of her view. He locked his eyes on the rear end of her car. Moments later he saw Lyric's car driving back into the apartments. He reversed his car back into the empty stall and wait.

"Man, something has gotta fold. I can't be posted up out here like this," he thought to himself, lighting the kush back up.

$$\$\$\$$

(THE ONE WHO THINKS HE KNOWS SOMETHING, DOESN'T KNOW WHAT HE THOUGHT HE DID.)

Lyric cautiously walked out of the store when Brittney drove away. She acted like she was using the pay phone scanning the scene. Once she was satisfied no one was paying her any attention, she "pink panthered" her way along the side of the store. The stench of urine made her hold her breath as she moved deftly through a trail of broken bottles and debris. Lyric peeked her head around the corner of the store. The black BMW sat in a stall facing the apartments.

She glanced behind her back to make sure she wasn't spotted by anyone. She stuck her hand into her jacket pocket wrapping her fingers around the chrome .32 automatic. Lyric looked at the gun before releasing the safety loading one into the chamber. She ducked down quickly sprinting to the stall next to the BMW. She lost her balance sliding on the slippery wet pavement. Lyric reached her hand out, resting it on the wall, as her left hand held the gun in a firm grip.

She took a deep breath exhaling through her lips before making her move.

Tron was feeling nice as the kush temporarily heightened his mood. He lay back in the driver's seat peering over the dashboard with eyes tighter than Jackie Chan's. Tron's first thought was to follow Lyric back into the apartments to see which one she walked inside. But if he was caught it would have been a folly on his part. His eyes darted to his side mirror sensing movement out of his peripheral vision. Tron glance quickly in his rearview mirror before casting his eyes back across the street.

"Man, this kush got me trippin'," he thought to himself, reaching for the remote control turning on the Alpine deck.

Before he attempted to turn the volume up, the back door on his passenger side flung open. It slammed into the brick stall with force rocking the whole car. Taken by surprise Tron had an astonishing look on his face, as a chrome automatic stare in his eyes.

"Why in the fuck are you following me?" Lyric hollered out with a furious expression on her face. "Huh nigga!"

Tron inched his hand towards the passenger seat where his .9mm Springfield with the blue finish sat, begging to save the day. Lyric peeped the play.

"Put your mutha fuckin' hands on the roof and face the front," she ordered, pressing the gun against the back of his head. "I'm gonna ask you one more time."

Tron felt the gun tremble in her hand as she spoke. "Why are you following me?" she asked again.

Tron knew a fearful woman would react instantly from emotions. He swallowed digesting the question she asked. "I was hoping you would lead me to Fast Blacc," He told her, staring at her through the rearview mirror. He saw the glittering fear that was in her eyes. Tron controlled his temper selecting his choice of words.

"When you dropped your cell phone last night, it was ringing when I picked it up. I peeped at the number and tripped out when I saw it was Fast Blacc," Tron continued, clenching his teeth in anger, "I wanted to ask you what was up with the nigga then, but you zoned out once you saw who it was," Tron explained, slightly shifting his hands on the roof of the car.

"Why are you looking for Fast Blacc?" Lyric asked, holding the gun against the back of his head.

"Check this out Lyric! If I wanted to do something to you, I could've got you last night at the room. I'm not finna tell you a mutha fuckin' thing, while you got that gun against my head," Tron said, narrowing his eyes in the rearview mirror.

Lyric thought back to when she woke up alone in the Super 8 Motel and found Tron's note on the table? "He could've done something to me then if he wanted to," Lyric told herself, lowering the gun.

Tron lowered his hands from the roof of the car massaging his arms. "Fast Blacc shot at me and my homeboy Redline. And he killed my cousin Bug," he said, noticing her wince when he mentioned Redline's name.

"You know Redline too?" she asked, combing her fingers through her hair unconsciously.

"Yeah, me and him go way back. Say Lyric, I think we need to go someplace else and talk. I been posted up out here a little bit too long. Ain't no telling who else saw you sneak up on me, cause I damn sure didn't," Tron said, looking at the same pretty smile he remembered from the gas station.

"My bad, but you had us scared. I think we need to talk this shit over too. We can go to my girlfriend's apartment," Lyric said, pointing across the street.

Once they made it to Brittney's place, Tron gave Lyric the full scoop on why he wanted to kill Fast Blacc. She was surprised to find out that the dude she saw laying in the warehouse was his relative. Lyric told him about Mona, starting from the hospital leading all the way to her death. She also told him about her plot she schemed up to get paid. Tron knew right away after hearing her plan, Lyric wasn't going to make it alive to spend a penny of the money.

"I was supposed to meet up with them at the Aquarium today."

"Alright! We can still do that, but I'm going with you," Tron told her, rubbing a hand across his chin. "I got a feeling you're gonna need me," he said, with malice spreading across his face.

Lyric set her plan back into motion. She texted Redline and Fast Blacc, (B@AQUARIUM HAV MY $). Lyric hopped in her car heading downtown with Tron following behind her.

(STARTING TROUBLE, ONLY MAKES ENEMIES, SO BE THE BIGGER PERSON AND WALK AWAY.)

CHAPTER 44

"PLOTTING WITH THE ENEMY"
(BILLAGE GREEN APARTMENTS)
HOUSTON, TEXAS

"Man, I thought you was gonna hit me up so we could handle this bitch?" Redline said.

"I call myself getting slick, by beatin' the hoe to the spot, but she ain't showed up yet," Fast Blacc told him, with his face twisted in a furious sneer.

"Do you think she's gonna show up?"

"Hell fuckin' yeah! For fifty-thousand dollars, who wouldn't show up." Fast Blacc said, gritting his teeth down on the tip of the Black & Mild. "Meet me up here at the Downtown Aquarium. I'm parked in the back," Fast Blacc continued.

"I'll be there in twenty minutes," Redline said, ending the call. Different thoughts began popping up in his mind like erections on adolescents. He drove down Telephone Road to a set of apartments called Village Green. Redline had to park his car just in case a law-abiding citizen decided to call the police. He looked around the parking lot locating his homegirl Ketha's car. He glanced back at his car, "Fuck!" he thought to himself, looking at the damage to the front end.

Instead of knocking on her door, Redline changed his mind and called. Ketha answered on the third ring. "Hello!"

"What's up girl you busy?" Redline asked, glancing towards the parking lot.

"N'all, just up here watching tv."

"Are you by yourself?" he asked.

"Damn nigga, why you askin' all these questions? If you're tryin' to come over just ask," Ketha said.

Redline knock on the door. "Hold on boy," Ketha told him, getting up to answer the door. Redline ended the call standing on the side of her door out of view. Ketha opened the door then sat back down on the couch.

Redline walked inside smiling. "You just open the door for anybody, huh?"

"Boy, your crazy ass is still, the only one who does that shit," Ketha told him, eyeing him up and down. "You almost got me! My brother told me you got out the other day."

"Yeah, I been out for a minute. Say Ketha, I don't have time to explain, but I need to use your car. My car is in the parking lot. Don't drive it until you hear from me, ok?" Redline explained, wiping the sweat from his forehead handing her his car keys.

"My keys are on the table," Ketha said, pointing towards the table. Redline grab the keys heading towards the door.

"Redline!" he stopped in his tracks turning around to face her. "You've been gone for eight years. Don't do nothing stupid that'll risk your life, or send you back to prison," Ketha said, standing to her feet giving him a big hug.

Redline swallowed the guilt in his throat walking out of the door. Ketha stood in her doorway staring at him until he was out of sight.

(BAD COMPANY CAN QUICKLY CHANGE A GOOD CHARACTER.)

CHAPTER 45

"SHOW TIME"
(DOWNTOWN AQUARIUM)
HOUSTON, TEXAS

Fast Blacc checked the text he received when he was talking to Redline. (B@AQUARIUM & HAV MY $) "Yeah I'm already here bitch. Ready and waiting," Fast Blacc said to himself, looking across the parking lot fingering the trigger on his Glock .380.

Everything began molding in the palm of his hands, and Fast Blacc didn't have time for mistakes. "NO MISTAKES NO MERCY NIGGA!" he thought to himself. A vehicle slowly creeped into the parking lot at a turtle's pace. Fast Blacc became alert sitting straight up in his seat. His right-hand clenched the Glock .380 in a death grip. The vehicle drove directly to the back of the parking lot towards him. His heart rate increased to a rapid beat. The vehicle reversed into a parking spot next to him. He turned sideways in his seat aiming his pistol at the driver of the vehicle.

Lyric had her mind on the fifty-thousand dollars turning into the parking lot of the Downtown Aquarium restaurant. She parked in the first empty spot her eyes notice. She'd been emotional since Amber's disappearance, and her mind wasn't focusing on any possible danger. Lyric hurried inside, sending Redline and Fast Blacc another text. (IM INSIDE). She glanced down at her watch calculating the hours left before her doctor's appointment.

She picked up a menu not to look suspicious, camouflaging her glances as if she were a little child. Lyric closed her eyes taking a deep breath, trying her best to calm her nerves. The hairs on her arm stood up.

Redline stepped out of the car placing his hands on the roof. When Fast Blacc saw it was Redline stepping out of the vehicle he put his gun away. "I need to smoke his ass right now," Fast Blacc thought to himself. The .380 tuck in his waistband behind his back began provoking him on.

"Has the bitch showed up yet?" Redline asked, gritting his teeth in rage at the sight of his enemy.

"Not that I know of," Fast Blacc told him, glancing down at his cell phone vibrating in his hand.

Redline looked up from his phone, "The little bitch is inside," he said.

"Well go handle your business. And if the bitch is slippin' when she comes out, I'll pop the hoe. If not, we'll follow her," Fast Blacc said, with his mouth twisted in anger. He knew Redline was a deceiver, and he refused to be tricked. His gaze drifted towards Redline walking inside of the restaurant.

Tron watched as Fast Blacc and Redline stood in the back of the parking lot talking. He wanted to peel Fast Blacc's head back right where he stood, and he would've if it wasn't for Redline being in the way. The sight of them made him wonder what was going on. Redline had already told Tron the scoop on Fast Blacc accepting the contract on his brother-n-law.

"Redline, what—the—fuck are you doing man?" Tron mumbled to himself, sitting in his car park in front of the restaurant.

Tron didn't care at all about Lyric, because his cards were already dealt. He decided to stay incognito to see how things played out. However, if a good opportunity came first to kill Fast Blacc, he was going to take it. Truth be told, killing someone in Downton Houston in broad daylight, wasn't on his list of smart things to do.

Lyric nervously waited with her eyes darting from the fish tanks to the stairs, watching as each person ascend. She held the glass of water with both hands trying to stop her hands from shaking. Redline and Fast Blacc's faces hung suspended in the forefront of her mind. Lyric felt her life was on the line. She reached for her cell phone dialing. The line rang a few times then it was answered.

"Hello!"

"I don't have time to explain what's going on. I want you to stay on the phone and don't say a word. Do you hear me?" Lyric asked, cutting her eyes towards the stairs.

"But what's-!"

"Don't worry about what's going on, just listen," Lyric interrupted. "I gotta go," Lyric said, peeping Redline walking up the stairs. Lyric sat her cell phone and keys on the table folding her hands to stop them from shaking. She was afraid. A warning mumbled in her brain as she whispered back at it in soundless despair.

(MALICE CAN BE HIDDEN BY DECEPTION, BUT MISDEEDS WILL BE REVEALED IN THE END.)

CHAPTER 46

"ALL ALONG"
(FEDERAL ROAD)
HOUSTON, TEXAS

Hollywood held the phone with a confusing look on her face. She didn't have a clue in the world what was going on. The way Lyric sounded over the phone had her on the edge, because she didn't tell if Lyric was alright or not. Hollywood covered the mouth end of the phone with her thumb, quietly listening.

"Do you have my money?" Lyric asked.

"Damn bitch, you don't waste no mutha fuckin' time, huh?" Redline told her.

When Hollywood heard Redline's voice, she pressed the phone harder up against her ear. She could sense there was something wrong.

"You didn't waste no time when you had Pee Wee killed, now did you?" Lyric snapped.

"Look here bitch, it don't matter what the fuck I had done. That's why I'm paying you this mutha fuckin' money. To—keep—your—mouth—shut," Redline said.

Tears began falling down Hollywood's face as she took a deep breath to steady her breathing. "How could he do this to me? After all these years we've been together," Hollywood thought to herself, trying to maintain her composure listening over the phone.

"Don't you feel real low down, having Hollywood's brother killed and your homeboy shot?" Lyric asked.

"I'm not paying you to tell me what the fuck I did, you understand! Here's your money, now shut the fuck up. If I hear anything about Amber, I'll let you know. She's probably dead, that's why you ain't heard from her," Redline said.

"How can you lay up with Hollywood like everything's all good, you paid Fast Blacc to kill her brother."

"You just won't shut up huh? Her brother fucked me over. He stopped paying me my money and decided to run off with my work. He felt since I was locked up, he couldn't be touched. Damn fool he was! The only thing hurt me, was when Flagg got shot. I got love for that nigga like a brother I never had. Fuck all this Oprah shit, just keep your end of the deal," Redline said angrily.

"You're a cold hearted no good mutha fucka," Lyric told him.

"Thank you!" Redline said politely.

Hollywood couldn't believe what she heard, even though the truth was exposed directly from the source. She brushed the unwanted tears away from her cheeks. Vindictive, devious, wicked, evil thoughts intersected her mind with ways for revenge. Hollywood was so dazed, lost deeply in her own thoughts she didn't hear Lyric talking to her.

"Hollywood! Hollywood! Are you still there?" Lyric asked, putting the fifty-thousand dollars in her purse.

"Yeah, I'm here Lyric," Hollywood muttered.

"Do you need any help getting rid of that no-good ass nigga?" Lyric asked, heading for the exit looking around wondering were Tron was at.

"N'all don't worry about it, I got everything under control. Thanks for everything. Call me if you need me, ok?" Hollywood said, ending the call. There was a deep pervasive sense of solitude in each of their brains.

(EVERYTHING YOU DO IN THE DARK WILL EVENTUALLY COME TO THE LIGHT.)

CHAPTER 47

"OUT OF SIGHT"
(DOWNTOWN AQUARIUM)
HOUSTON, TEXAS

Tron's gaze followed Redline as he walked towards the back of the parking lot. He didn't see Fast Blacc smoothly disappear behind the tinted windows of the Buick Regal. Momentarily, Lyric made her exit with fifty-thousand dollars in her purse tucked under her armpit. She headed for her car dashing her eyes across the parking lot nervously, as if she had stolen something.

Tron watched her drive away as a burgundy Buick Regal pulled out of the parking lot right behind her. He reclined his seat all the way back when Redline and Fast Blacc drove by. Little did he know, Fast Blacc was fresh on Lyric's tail instead of riding shotgun with Redline like he thought. Tron gave them a little distance before beginning his pursuit.

He hoped Redline knew what he was doing. Tron figured they were going to follow Lyric when she left. Redline's car was a lane over, two cars behind Lyric. Tron merged into the same lane Lyric was driving in. He allowed a good two car distance between them. Lyric hopped off I-45 taking the US 59 exit. Redline's car continued driving straight.

Tron tapped on his brakes lightly reducing his speed, staying inconspicuous. The traffic flowed smooth without any congestion. Tron glanced to his left at the Third Ward neighborhood. His mind instantly flashed back to his days of skipping school and stealing cars. A faint uneven smile crossed his face flickering before it disappeared.

Redline hopped on HWY 288 heading towards 610 South. He exited on Old Spanish Trail. Tron made a left turn at the light staying on their tail. Redline made another left turn, this time on Allegany by club Reminisce. Tron waited in the middle of the intersection allowing them a little distance. He sped up when they made a left turn at the corner on Dixie. When Tron made the left turn Redline was gone.

"FUCK!" Tron said, frustrated with himself for losing them.

He quickly noticed a group of hoodlums standing in front of a building to his right. Tron glance towards the motel on his left and saw the brake lights shining on the car Redline was driving. He drove down the block and made a U-turn, parking on the corner by a Ralston liquor store. His mind wondered why they stopped following Lyric and drove to this destination. Tron let the thought linger in his brain.

(WICKED WAYS CAN NEVER BE OVERLOOKED, THEY CAN ONLY LEAD TO DEATH.)

CHAPTER 48

"BLINDED BY LUST AND GREED"
(11162 BRAEFOREST DR.)
HOUSTON, TEXAS

Lyric didn't even bother with checking her rearview mirror for a possible tail. If only she would have paid attention to the burgundy Buick Regal that was following her, instead of the fifty-thousand dollars in her purse, maybe her life would have been prolonged. She turned into her driveway pressing the automatic garage door opener. She squeezed her car in between the new furniture and new appliances cluttering her garage. She struggled with the car door as it barely open wide enough for her to wiggle her shapely body through. She lowered the garage door with the touch of a finger then walk inside.

A burgundy Buick Regal slowly crept by as the garage door came to a close. Lyric sat down at the kitchen table emptying the money and other contents out of her purse. The path to her own destruction would come from her being blinded by lust and greed. She stared at the money as her thoughts scattered momentarily. She found tears forming in her eyes picturing her and Amber in one of their intimate moments.

Lyric glance around as words whispered a warning in her mind she didn't understand. She fought against the fear washing through her. Being pregnant by a madman that wanted to kill her was a hard pill to swallow. She looked down at her watch thinking about her appointment with Dr. Howard. With over two hours to kill, she grabbed the money off the table walking into her bedroom. She tossed the money on the dresser then laid across her king size bed dozing off to sleep.

(CARELESS DECISIONS CAN LEAD TO AN EARLY GRAVE.)

CHAPTER 49

"STRAIGHT TO THE POINT"
(THE GOLDEN MOTEL)
HOUSTON, TEXAS

Redline received a text from Reno right before he hooked up with Fast Blacc. Reno had wanted him to come to the Golden Motel as soon as possible. Redline was leery about returning to the scene after the shooting. He parked Ketha's car right next to Reno's surveying the scene like an owl. After feeling comfortable he quickly made his way inside. Reno signaled with the wave of his hand for Redline to come inside through the back. He knew if he would have stayed instead of leaving, this situation would have never happened.

"I knew I should have stayed just in case he came back," Reno said, glancing at the security monitors.

"Did the laws show up?" Redline asked, rubbing a hand under his chin unconsciously.

"Yes, my sister called them when she heard the shooting. The police asked all types of questions. You know, the basic stuff. Did I know him? What was he doing around here? I just told them he came around a lot selling drugs to the drug addicts that hung around the motel," Reno explained, getting up from the chair walking towards the security monitors.

Redline notice the security monitors for the very first time since he'd been coming to the motel. The first monitor was frozen on the entranceway, and the game room building across the street. The second monitor captured the entire right side, directly in front of room 25, his honeycomb hideout. The last monitor displayed the left side of the motel. Redline's mind quickly registered.

"Did they ask about the cameras?" he asked, with his heart hammering and the blood pounding dully in his ears. Redline never thought about the cameras that were position around the motel, while he was exchanging hot lead with his mysterious foe.

"The lead detective did. Once he saw the camera pointing towards the room Bo was found in, he became excited," Reno explained.

Redline nervously bit down on his teeth. "He asked to check out the monitors after he saw the camera. When he saw the screens, he started smiling. But when I told him there were no recordings, and the cameras were on a direct line to the monitors, his smile quickly disappeared," Reno explained, noticing Redline's worried expression change into relief.

Redline inhaled a deep breath blowing air out between his lips. "Reno, I owe you more than I can explain my nigga," Redline told him, walking towards the security monitors.

"My friend, anything I can do for you consider it done. You never showed me or my family any type of disrespect. So, by that alone I look at you as a brother," Reno said, extending his hand out for Redline to shake.

They both exchange glances as Redline swallow hard against the feeling coursing through him. Redline shook Reno's hand with a firm grip. Movement on one of the monitors caught his attention in his peripheral. He turned his head towards the screens leaning down studying the vehicle driving up to the game room.

"Ain't this a bitch!" Redline said, wiping the screen trying to get a better look.

"That's the same car Bo was in when I called you this morning," Reno told him.

"Are you sure?" Redline asked, with his face less than a few inches away from the surveillance monitor.

"I can't say I'm for sure, but it looks just like it," Reno said, gazing at the screen.

"Can you zoom in a little bit?" Redline asked, looking for bullet holes in the windshield. He stared at the lone figure with a menacing look on his face. There were no bullet holes in the windshield so Redline figured he had it replaced.

"Do you think that's him?" Reno asked, looking down at the back of Redline's head which was blocking the monitor.

Redline heard Reno, but his mind and sight were locked on his target. He didn't respond as revenge began churning in his brain like a witch's brew. The sole figure turned around and face the motel. It was like he knew someone was watching him. Guilt was eating away at his conscience. The hairs on the back of Redline's neck stood at attention.

"That's him!" Redline said, as his forefinger slowly followed his enemy on the surveillance monitor.

"What are we going to do?" Reno asked.

Redline turned around to face him with eyes glinting with anger. "I'm gonna finish what they started, and send him to meet his bitch ass homeboy," Redline told him, as his eyes shine like black glass.

Reno swallowed, gazing at him blankly. "The only thing I need you to do, is keep doing what you've been doing."

"And what's that my friend?" Reno asked, trying to evaluate his disposition.

"Keepin' your eyes glued to that screen. Let me know if you see anyone moving around besides me. Especially the laws!" Redline said, glancing back at the screen watching his foe walk inside of the game room.

"Well, like you always say. Bet that!" Reno responded, taking a seat in front of the monitors rubbing his hands together before rubbing his knees. Unprovoked violence has never been his forte.

But Reno was far from inexperienced when it came down to protecting himself or his family. He watched Redline make a beeline across the street. Next Redline disappeared behind a brown, four door Park Avenue with tinted windows.

"I hope you have this figured out my friend," Reno said to himself, inhaling then blowing air out of his nostrils.

(THOSE WHO HATE WITHOUT REASONS EXCEED IN

NUMBERS. MANY ARE HATERS WITHOUT A CAUSE.)

$$$

About a block away, the individual who initiated Redline's irrational thinking, which leads to his misdeeds and mishaps, stood at a corner pay phone watching his every move. Redline was unaware of being observed once again. His mind and sight were locked in a tunnel vision, anticipating his next kill. There was no threatening or disrespectful words exchanged between them. The problem he had with Redline was well known across the world. It's called JEALOUSLY! Two people in the same game moving at their own pace, chasing their inner addiction.

He stared at Redline with interest wondering what was about to take place? And with who? Different thoughts tap dance in his brain as he peered at Redline walking towards the side of the building. He reached for the Black & Mild resting behind his right ear. Slowly between his thumb and index finger, he loosened up the tobacco with a rolling motion from top to bottom. Placing the Black & Mild in his mouth, he poured out eight ounces of Welch's grape soda.

He glanced around momentarily before pouring the purple syrup into the 1-liter bottle of grape soda. He coated the Black & Mild with the remaining drops, throwing the empty prescription bottle on the ground. He lit the Black & Mild glancing at the tip burning like a candle. The syrup sizzle underneath the flame. He blew it out then inhale deeply.

He grabbed the grape soda sitting upside down on top of the pay phone. Twisting the top open, he slowly poured the controlled substance into a big white Styrofoam cup filled with crush ice. The ice crackled with seeming pleasure as the cup was filled. He downed the first cup licking his lips. The taste was the best thing next to pussy. After pouring the rest of the substance into the awaiting cup of ice, he threw the bottle away. Taking a sip savoring the taste, he started walking with his eyes on the building Redline eased behind.

(EVEN THE WATCHERS ARE BEING WATCHED.)

$$$

Redline stared at the car from around the corner of the building. He noticed the bullet holes in the grill, and the damage on the left side. He saw a homeless man digging through his shopping cart full of worldly possessions. That's when an idea popped in his head.

"Look out old school!" Redline hollered out. The old man studied Redline suspiciously before nodding his head. "Let me holla at you for a minute," Redline said, the old man looked around for any type of threat before approaching him.

"What's up Adrain?" the old man asked. Redline's heart rate instantly increased and his blood pound through his veins upon hearing his government name. His hand immediately reached for the nickel plated .45.

"Hold on Adrain! Hold up now! If I knew you were gonna act like this, I would've stayed my ass over there," the old man said, trying to defuse the situation before it blew up. "One thing I do know, being on point runs through the Jones bloodline," the old man said, with his hands reaching for the sky.

Redline stared at the old man with a quizzical look on his face. "You look just like your pops when we were running the streets back in the gap (MANY YEARS AGO)," the old man said, with a smile on his face.

Redline snapped with a sense of realization after looking beyond the old man's appearance. He came to recognition that he knew him.

"Damn Cowboy! I almost shot that hat off your head," Redline said, relieved of the moment.

"Boy, you had the old man shook up for a minute there," Cowboy told him, blowing air between his lips wiping sweat from his forehead. "By the way things look, I don't think it's a good time to be reminiscing about the past," Cowboy said, eyeing the gun that was begging for attention.

"Cowboy I need your help. All I want to hear is yes or no. Do you know that nigga who drives that dookie brown Park Avenue with the tinted windows?" Redline asked, motioning in the direction of the car with a head nod.

Cowboy turned around picking up an empty beer can. He glanced at the car as he rose up. "Yeah!" he answered.

"I got two-hundred for you. All I want you to do is, go tell that fool somebody is messing with his car. No more no less."

Cowboy let the words Redline said saturate through his brain before answering. "Let's go with it!" Cowboy told him, extending his arm towards Redline with his palm open.

"That's what I'm talkin' about! no questions asked," Redline said, handing Cowboy an extra hundred for not being nosey. Cowboy slam dunked the money deep into his pocket along with the lint and dirt. He adjusted his hat walking inside of the game room thinking about the very first time he ran into J Man...

"Nigga, get that bitch ass basket out of the mutha fuckin' way!" J Man yelled, as Cowboy pushed his junkyard on wheels across the street. J Man held his hand down on the car horn yelling at the top of his lungs. Something fell from underneath Cowboy's basket and he stopped to pick it up. J Man jumped out of his car high and frustrated from being broke.

"Didn't I tell you to get this bitch ass basket outta the street!" J Man hollered out, as he shoved the basket across the street with all his might. The shopping cart crashed into the curb, and all of Cowboy's possessions went everywhere.

"What's up you old mutha fucka!? You wanna do something?" J Man yelled.

Cowboy was about to fix his lips to say something. J Man shoved him so hard with both hands he landed on his butt. Cowboy fell back and busted his head on the concrete. He reached up and felt the back of his head. His hand came back completely covered in blood. Cowboy wanted to hop up and retaliate, but he was smart enough to know he didn't have a chance. He gazed grimly from the ground. J Man got back into his car and sped away...

"What the fuck do you want, Old bum ass nigga! Say old man, do you hear me?" J Man asked, poking his finger in Cowboys chest.

Cowboy snapped out of his daze with a furious look on his face. "I just wanted to tell you somebody's fuckin' with your car," Cowboy told him, as a smile began to register upon his face.

"You better hope ain't nobody fuckin' with my shit, dumpster smellin' ass nigga," J Man said, placing his drink down on the table rushing outside. Cowboy took another deep breath heading towards the bar.

"I might as well get me a couple of drinks under my belt. In case he comes back trippin'," Cowboy mumbled to himself, walking towards the bar.

Outside, J Man walked around his car looking to see if anything was wrong. He leaned down noticing his back tire was flat. Out of anger, J Man started kicking the flat tire repeatedly as profanity flew from his lips. He opened the trunk so he could get the spare. With both hand on the trunk of the car, he stopped in mid-motion. J Man looked around with a feeling of being watched. Instead of following his first thought, he bent down ignoring the warning. While trying to retrieve a small hydraulic jack from behind the speaker box, someone else had other plans.

"Remember me?" Redline asked, with his nickel plated .45 aiming right in the back of J Man's head. J Man turned around gaping at Redline. He recognized the Al B sure look alike instantly.

"Man I—!" those were the only words that escape J Man's mouth. The .45 automatic sounded off like a cannon slamming into his face. The inside of the trunk was coated with blood. His body lay lifeless on top of the speaker box. The left side of his face and cranium were blown away. Redline walked away discreetly as possible, with the eyes of three individuals watching him. He controlled his own destiny, and there were only two individuals he had to answer to. One is the almighty GOD. The other is his better half, Hollywood.

(ALL MISDEEDS WILL BE JUDGED, AND YOU WILL BE
HELD ACCOUNTABLE.)

$$$

The sound of the gun blast startled Tron. He sat witnessing the quick flame exit the gun, along with the person that squeezed the trigger. Quickly, he started his car and made a U-turn heading towards

Interstate 288. His mind-juggled around thoughts as he merged onto the freeway, skillfully blending in with traffic. His mind was puzzled on a few things. What stood out the most was, where the fuck was Fast Blacc? And how could Redline be stupid enough to trust his enemy after he already tried to kill his girl?

Tron shook his head taking the US 59 exit heading North. He dialed Renee's number wondering why Lil' Branon hadn't answered any of his calls or text. The call went straight to the voicemail on the first ring. Tron called back again before trying Lil' Branon's number. His phone went straight to the voice mail too. A bloodcurdling feeling rush over his body making him automatically think about Lyric. He had completely forgot about her during his surveillance of Redline. Tron slice through traffic precisely. He exited US 59 hopping on I-45 North heading towards Greenspoint.

He turned on his hazard lights pressing his foot harder on the gas pedal. He zipped past vehicles as the speedometer inched over a hundred miles an hour. The freeway lights shone off the body of the black on black 745i, speeding through the night closing in on its destination. Tron called Lyric expecting the worst but hoping the best until his situation blows over. The more he thought about Lyric, his brain pondered more on the whereabouts of Fast Blacc. An old song by the late rapper Fat Pat (R.I.P) cross his mind. "FRIENDS AND FOES TURN ENEMIES."

Tron knew a friend was the worst enemy a person could have. He learned that from firsthand experience. A friend would know where to look, where an enemy would never suspect. Tron exited Greens Road making a right turn at the traffic light, heading to Lyric's girlfriend's apartment.

(EVERY SITUATION CALLS FOR LOGICAL THINKING.)

CHAPTER 50

"LIVING NIGHTMARE"
(11162 BRAESFOREST DR.)
HOUSTON, TEXAS

L yric lay across her king size canopy bed dreaming about the hair-raising experience she encountered with Fast Blacc...

$$$

"Look out Mona, don't worry about a mutha fuckin' thing. I got everything under control, you hear me?" Fast Blacc explained over the cell phone, with his eyes dancing back and forth from the rearview mirror to the road.

Lyric lay bound by a cord in the backseat with both hands tied behind her back to her feet. She quietly listened to Fast Blacc talk over the phone, while she swiftly, but calmly worked on loosening the restraints.

"Just keep following me. I got a spot out there in Killeen where we can get rid of the bitch," Fast Blacc said, ending the call. He wiped the sweat from his forehead. He held the steering wheel steady with his left knee, reaching for the vanilla extract bottle filled with formaldehyde.

Fast Blacc inserted a More cigarette into the clear substance. The smell instantly invaded Lyric's nostrils as she tried to blow away the fumes.

The fumes became thicker as they drowned all hopes of clean air. Lyric inhaled a rush of the deadly fumes. The fumes traveled quickly to her lungs...then began squeezing. Lyric's eyes widened. She tired to scream but no sound came from her mouth. Tears descended down her cheeks rapidly as her life came to an end. Her mind screamed her last please. "Noooo!"...

$$$

Lyric raised up with a sudden jerk, scanning her bedroom. When her brain realized she was safe at home in her own bed, she sat up reaching for the remote control. Turning on the television, she surfed through the channels stopping on an episode of Housewives of Houston. She rubbed her temples trying to calm the headache that was creeping up.

"KNOCK KNOCK KNOCK KNOCK KNOCK!" Lyric glanced down at the clock on her nightstand. Ever since she moved to her new home someone was trying to sell her something. It was either that, or the Jehovah's Witnesses every other day. She sluggishly moved her feet getting out of bed. Lyric remembered the appointment she had with Dr. Howard as soon as she stood to her feet.

"KNOCK KNOCK KNOCK!"

"Yeah Yeah Yeah," Lyric muttered under her breath, sliding her feet across the flush polished marble floor. She stood on her tip toes peeking through the peephole. A smile darted across her face when she saw the pink teddy bear. The only person who knew where she stayed was Brittney.

"Who is it?" Lyric asked, opening the door with a delightful grin on her face.

"SURPRISE! SURPRISE! SURPRISE!" a male voice sang, imitating the late Jim Neighbors from the Gomer Pyle show. Lyric's mind was focused on the numerous balloons with "I LOVE YOU" all over them.

"Here you go ma'am," the man said, quickly and smoothly making his way inside without alarming Lyric. He handed her the bouquet of balloons which were covering his upper body. Lyric wrestled with the bundle of balloons. When she had them situated, she turned around to thank the delivery man.

"AAAHHH!" Lyric screamed out, making a sudden dash for the front door.

Fast Blacc kicked and closed the front door close with brute force making pictures fall from the wall. Lyric slip down on her rear changing directions once the door slammed shut. She quickly turned over running. Her feet were moving fast sliding across the marble floor. Fast Blacc reached down to grab her legs. Lyric kicked up forcefully connecting with his nose.

"BIIITCH!" Fast Blacc hollered out, reaching for his bleeding nose.

Lyric snatched off her socks before grabbing a life size replica of Barrack Obama's head. She threw the head at Fast Blacc. The statue collided with his left knee sending him straight down to the floor hollering out in pain. Fast Blacc reached for his Glock .380 squeezing off a quick shot. The bullet pierce through her left leg. Lyric screamed out in pure agony dragging herself along the hallway floor. A heavy trail of blood marked her path.

Fast Blacc stood to his feet looking around for something to stop the blood from flowing out of his nose. He reached down picking up one of her socks. He glanced down at the droplets of blood on the marble floor. Fast Blacc looked up as Lyric was trying to turn the corner. He ran and grabbed a handful of her hair nudging the pistol aggressively in her face.

"Fuck you nigga! And this is for Amber bitch!" Lyric screamed out, before spitting in his face.

"NO MISTAKES NO MERCY BITCH!" he growled, shoving the Glock .380 deeply down her throat pulling the trigger.

He stood up and place another shot right through her forehead. Fast Blacc rushed a check quickly through the house in search of a bathroom. Once he located one, he began grabbing a few towels. He searched under the sink for any type of cleaning substance. He snatched up a bottle of Clorox pouring some over one of the towels. Fast Blacc check the bottom of his shoes for any traces of blood. He back tracked scanning over the way he came. He carefully stepped over

Lyric's dead body. He wiped up the blood spots with the towel. Fast Blacc repeated the process one more time backing himself towards the front door. He stood up preparing to leave. He stopped in mid stride. He took a few steps and grabbed the bouquet of balloons before walking out of the door.

(EVERY GET-AWAY WILL EVENTUALLY COME TO AN END.)

CHAPTER 51

"FOUND OUT"
(FEDERAL ROAD)
HOUSTON, TEXAS

Redline hopped out of a cab a couple of blocks away from his house. The cab driver peered in his rearview mirror with suspicious thoughts, watching Redline walk across the street. Redline picked up his pace eliminating the distance between his enemies and getting closer to his haven. Flashbacks of numerous ways that things should have been taken care of toyed with his mind.

He glanced to his left. A red Nissan Altima turned into a driveway. Redline wonder did Fast Blacc handle his business killing Lyric. She was one problem he could do without. Redline looked up and saw Hollywood's Lexus SUV park in the driveway. Taking a deep breath, he walked into the house shaking his head. He knew Hollywood would never understand the actions he took. He did what he felt had to be done.

Even though Hollywood knew the code of the streets and respected it by all means. But being betrayed by the one you love, for killing someone who was bound through blood, are two different aspects of the game. "THIS IS A MAN'S WORLD!" James Brown sang in the forefront of his mind crossing the threshold to their home. "AND IT WOULDN'T BE A DAMN THING, WITHOUT A WOMAN'S TOUCH!" Redline smiled as the mouth watering aroma captured his sense of smell. He closed the front door leaning back up against it.

It felt good to do the small things he never knew he would miss. The smell of a good home cooked meal was one of them. Being able to go and come as he pleased was the main thing he missed besides Hollywood. The last ten years of his life jumped out at him in episodes...

$$\$\$\$$$

"All rise! This is the state of Texas vs Adrian Jones. Foreman have you and the jury come to a verdict?"

"Yes, we have your honor!" the foreman answered, holding the folded-up piece of paper.

The foreman handed Redline's life over to the judge on a small piece of paper. "The people of the jury have found you...guilty!" The judge said sternly...

"Jones, pack your shit you're on the chain headed to TDC!" a county jail officer yelled over the intercom...

"Say youngster! Can you wake up for a minute so I can use the restroom?" The old man asked, who was handcuffed to Redline as they rode on a bluebird bus headed to prison...

"Take off all of your clothes! Now raise your hands above your head! Raise up your nutsacks! Turn around bend over and spread your asscheeks!" the redneck guard yelled out, with a big fat dip of snuff in his mouth, and a nigger hater scowl etched on his face.

"Roll 334! Enjoy your stay boy!" the redneck correctional guard said, as he pushed Redline into the cell. The cell door closed with a loud clank when the steel bars slammed shut...

"Hey Michael, can I get your autograph? Oh! I'm sorry! I thought you were Michael from off of the Good Times," Hollywood teased when she picked Redline up from Huntsville, Texas when he was released from prison...

$$\$\$\$$$

"Hey baby, are you alright?" Hollywood asked, looking up at him leaning against the front door. When she didn't get him to answer, she stepped up on her tip toes passionately kissing him on the lips. She felt him responding when his dick throbbed against her leg. Hollywood put a smile on her face.

"Is that the only way I can get your attention?" Hollywood asked, with a smirk on her face.

"N'all baby, I just zoned out thinking how lucky I was to have you in my life," Redline told her, wrapping his arms around her waist. "I know we've been squabblin' since I been home. But baby, I promise you this bullshit will be over within a few days. I want our relationship to stay the same between us. Everything I do is for you. Ain't no questions about it." Redline leaned down placing a kiss softly on her forehead.

Hollywood cried on the inside. It took everything she had not to let the tears flow down her face. Every part of her body flowed with love for Redline. A love that was built upon trust, time, heartaches, and a lake full of tears. Hollywood overlooked a lot of small problems she had with him. She knew a man would be a man regardless of who they're with.

She also knew when to draw the line and put her foot down. "And I'm here for you baby! So never let your mind entertain thoughts other than that. I'll make sure our foundation stays strong throughout the storm," she said, not giving away a clue that she knew what was going on.

Hollywood felt his eyes roaming over her body. "So, is that the new you?"

"What are you talkin' about?" Redline asked, with a puzzle look on his face.

"I'm talking about how you're lusting behind my back," Hollywood said, lowering her head laughing. "I guess you thought I didn't know," she said.

"Damn, you got eyes in your ass too?" Redline joked.

Hollywood looked over her shoulder with a smile. Certain things about a person will never change, and the love she had for Redline was one of them. "TILL DEATH DO US APART," she thought to herself walking into the kitchen.

Hollywood's black widow instincts began webbing up quickly. She prepared three T-bone steaks well-done exactly the way he liked. It would have been a very easy task to just poison his food and watch him die. But Hollywood had a special arrangement set up for the two of them. The smell of the steaks snatched her brain free from her vindictive thoughts. Hollywood opened the oven checking the meal, making sure it was done. Satisfied with her superb cooking skills, she closed the oven door.

Right when she removed her oven mitts a cold chill flowed over her body. She peered down at the reflection staring back at her from the smoke grey glass on the oven's door. "Wee Pee!" Hollywood said out loud. She turned around, only to see Redline sitting on the couch watching television with his back facing her. Even though she was standing right in front of the hot oven, she rubbed her hands up and down her arms chasing away the sudden chill.

"I already know Wee Pee! I already-know," she said silently. "Redline, dinner is ready baby!" Hollywood hollered out, with her thoughts going into overdrive. Her fury was well hidden.

It was difficult for her to accept being deceived by the love of her life. The words, "TILL DEATH DO US APART," whispered from somewhere in the back of her conscience.

Hollywood gazed at Redline eating his meal like it was his last one on earth. Ever since he'd been home Hollywood noticed how fast he ate all of his meals, like his food was about to run off.

"Then again, who knows. This may be his last meal," Hollywood thought to herself, cutting into her steak.

Her thoughts began scrambling. The image of Redline standing in the mall staring at Fast Blacc was foremost in her mind. A hint of mischievousness flashed briefly in her dark pupils. Hollywood cut a piece off her steak and hand fed it to Redline. He gladly accepted, sucking the steak sauce off her finger.

"Boy, you better stop before you get me started," she said, wiping away the steak sauce from the corner of his mouth with her index finger. Redline grabbed her hand licking the sweet honey steak sauce off her fingers.

"I don't care! Cause once I get you started, you'll be screaming for me to stop," Redline smiled, standing to his feet snatching on the waistband of his pants.

Hollywood watched him walk back into the living room. Living life without him sank deeper into the silence of her brain. Tears began building up behind her closed eyelids, Anger welled up within, but she quickly brought it under control. Her anger would only blind her thoughts, and she needed to keep her vision clear, if she wanted to begin planning her vengeance against her deceiving lover. The question "WHY?" remained the one answer she was seeking. Before the storm blows over, her answer will be brought to the light. Hollywood wiped her hands on a dish towel before starting the dishwasher.

Grabbing a knife out of the kitchen drawer, she gripped it tightly in her hand. Her heart hammered with adrenaline and anticipation as a smile spread across her face. Each step she took closer to Redline her adrenaline sped through her arteries and veins on its own mission. Hollywood stood right behind him as he watched the Houston Texans put a pounding on the Baltimore Ravens. She placed the knife against his neck under his chin.

"I guess you thought I would never find out. How could you do this to me?" Hollywood asked, pressing the knife harder against his throat.

"Baby calm-!" he started to say.

"Shut the fuck up while I'm talking," she said, with her mouth inches away from his ear. "Let me do the talking. All I want you to do is nod yes or no. Do you understand me?" Hollywood asked, making him move to the end of the couch. She held the knife firmly against his neck.

Redline's heart began pumping faster than the thoughts racing through his mind. "How did she find out?" was the first thought that came to his mind.

He felt the knife move underneath his chin as Hollywood maneuver her body on top of his. The look on her face sent a jolt of fear rushing throughout his body.

"Now I'm gonna ask you this one time, and one time only," Hollywood said, applying pressure with the knife positioning her right foot on the floor. Redline tried to talk, but discomposure caught the lie before it escaped his mouth.

"Did she suck your dick?" Hollywood asked, raising her body up grabbing a handful of his crotch. He felt her hand rub up and down the length of his dick. Worry instantly left his body. Redline nodded his head up and down. He was happy it was a false alarm.

"Did she suck your dick better than me," Hollywood asked, batting her eyelashes biting down on her bottom lip seductively.

Redline shook his head side to side implying no. His blood rushed to the head of his dick faster than Serena Williams' serve. Hollywood continued to fondle him through his pants. She aimed to please, while all along plotting to destroy at the same time.

"What comes around goes around," she thought to herself, dancing her tongue slowly in his mouth. Redline felt the knife move away from his neck. Hollywood reached over setting it down on the coffee table.

He glimpsed at the butter knife rubbing his hand across his throat. Hollywood's hot tongue took his thoughts away from the butter knife leaving a long damp trail down his stomach. Sex was every man's weakness, and Hollywood was taking advantage of his. She unbuckled his belt then unzipped his pants releasing her prey. His dick popped out of his boxer shorts ready for trouble. A sneaky smile appeared across her face before she dove headfirst into his lap.

(LOVE AND PLEASURE CAN DISTORT A PERSON'S WAY OF THINKING. SO, DON'T BE SURPRISED, BEWARE.)

CHAPTER 52

"SOMETHING AIN'T RIGHT"
(KELLY COURT APARTMENTS)
HOUSTON, TEXAS

Tron turned into Kelly Court apartments with the same thought tapping at his brain. Where was Lil' Branon? Two boppers (females) stared at their reflection in the mirror tinted windows of the black 745i with the same thought running through their minds. "Who was the driver?" and "Who was the driver going to see?"

Tron peered at their fat asses in his rearview mirror with lustful thoughts on his mind. He dialed Renee's number as he got closer to her apartment. Looking around the parking lot, he located a parking spot. He looked around watchfully before ending the call stepping out of his car. Tron glanced briefly at the setting noticing a few heads turn in his direction. He casually fired up a Black & Mild striding across the parking lot.

The smell of weed and barbecue floated throughout the air making his stomach growl. He thought about the last time he had eaten something, which was well over twelve hours ago. He inhaled the addictive substance that was coated around the Black & Mild. The promethazine and codeine filled his lungs instantly curbing his hunger. He exhaled glancing back at the two dudes he saw watching him when he stepped out of his car. They were in the midst of their own conversation as he turned into the breezeway on his left.

The windows on Renee's apartment were slightly covered with frost. He knocked on the door inhaling deeply from the tip of the Black & Mild. Tron glanced down the breezeway being cautiously observant of his surroundings. He grabbed his cell phone pressing send redialing Renee's number. The call went straight to her voice mail. He knocked on the door again.

Tron looked around checking to see if he was being watched. He reached out turning the doorknob. The cold doorknob turned in his hand. The door opened. Then he peeked to his left and right before entering the apartment. He closed the door behind him. The first thing he noticed was the drop in the temperature.

"Look out Renee!" Tron yelled out, resting a hand on the black .9mm that was tuck in the waistband of his pants. "Damn it's cold in here," he thought to himself, looking around the apartment. He walked towards the bedroom.

"Renee!" he hollered out again, crossing the threshold of the bedroom. There was no one in the bedroom. He checked the bathroom. The bathroom was empty. He checked the bathtub before walking back out. His cell phone vibrated in his hand sending a sudden chill fluttering across his body. Tron glanced down at the screen and a smile ripple across his face, when he saw Tera's number staring back at him. He checked the closet while answering the call.

"What's up Miss Lady?" He answered.

"By now you should already know," Tera said, sounding seductive and sexy.

"I feel you lil' momma. I'm out here in H-town right now, but when I get back to K-town (Killeen) I'll hit you up," Tron said, sitting down on the bed placing a Black & Mild in his mouth. He pulled out his cigarette lighter blazing up the soothing laced cigar.

"I don't know how long I can keep this pussy dripping wet, waiting on you. I hope you make it here before my batteries wear out," Tera moaned through the phone. Tron instantly grabbed his crotch.

"Don't worry, I'll buy you a battery charger if they do. I'll get back with you sexy, ok,"' Tron said, inhaling the Black & Mild.

"Ok boy, but don't keep me waiting all night," Tera told him, blowing a kiss into the phone.

Tron ended the call standing to his feet. The cigarette lighter fell out of his hand onto the floor, bouncing underneath the bed. When he kneeled grabbing his cigarette lighter, he saw something else. Tron jumped up from the floor slapping at his arm. A big cockroach was crawling up his arm towards his neck. He started swatting at his neck with both hands spinning and hopping around the room. The cockroach flew off his neck crashing into the wall. The way Tron was acting it was hard to tell who feared who. He walked over to the roach stomping on it.

"Mutha fucka!" Tron grunted through his teeth. He glanced at his watch calculating his next move. There still wasn't a clue in his mind on where Lil' Branon and Renee were at. He wiped his prints off the doorknob exiting the apartment.

The chill bumps disappeared from his body stepping into the warm air of the night. Tron pressed the automatic starter button on his key chain, making the BMW come to life. The headlights shined bright, illuminating his body, casting his shadow on the apartment's brick walls. Tron hopped in his car with finding a few answers on his mind.

(MISTAKES ARE MADE DUE TO LACK OF THINKING, AND BEING DISTRACTED CAN LEAD TO FAILURE.)

CHAPTER 53

"CLOSE CALL"
(ALFREDA'S SOUL FOOD)
HOUSTON, TEXAS

Fast Blacc sat in a diner behind a plate filled with good old-fashioned soul food by Alfreda's. Needing a place to settle down he decided to stop and feed his neglected stomach. His appetite for food was replaced with More menthol cigarettes soaked in formaldehyde. He looked down at the pork chops smothered in gravy, white rice topped with butter, fresh greens with slices of fat backs and corn bread.

Even though his mind was focused on smoking a good sherm, the aroma from the food gained control over his corrupt judgement. He bit into the pork chop like a savage beast. He bit his tongue from chewing so fast, but that didn't stop his jaws from moving. Fast Blacc glanced out the window at the cars darting by heading to their destinations. His mind wandered back to Renee for reasons unknown. Something was beckoning his brain to return to her apartment. He continued eating his meal lost in a daze.

The image of Renee laid across her bed with her shorts resting between her ass began playing with his conscience. Fast Blacc was oblivious of the stares from other patrons. They were unable to enjoy their meal because of his rugged appearance. Once his plate was cleaned, he tackled both of his side dishes. He went to work on a side helping of peach cobbler. After he washed down his food with a glass of iced tea, he placed a tip on the table and made his exit.

He glanced around the parking lot before hopping into his car. As he turned the ignition, his addiction whispered in his mind before the engine started. Fast Blacc reached for a More cigarette drowning it into the pungent liquid. His car idled quietly as the sounds of The Grit Boys murmured through the speakers. He blazed up the sherm blowing out the flame inhaling furiously, instantly escaping reality. The image of Lyric crawled across his brain from a distance. He smiled, thinking back upon his latest remorseless murder. He exhaled the thick sherm smoke. "NO MISTAKES NO MERCY NIGGA!" he said to himself, taking another drag placing his car in reverse.

The smoke hung thick within the car. "No Mistakes No Mercy Nigga," were the words that continued to play over and over in his mind. Despite the fair warning, Fast Blacc took another hit from the sherm heading straight to Renee's apartment in Fifth Ward. The ride from Third Ward to Fifth Ward took him thirty minutes instead of fifteen, because the mind-boggling drug slows down everything but time. The closer he got to Kelly Court apartments his heart hammered hard against his chest, anticipating the excitement of returning to the scene. "No Mistakes No Mercy Nigga," bounced from one side of his brain to the other exiting I-10 West. His jugular vein pulsed as his blood race through his body.

Fast Blacc glanced around when he turned into the apartments. He quickly noticed a Harris County Sheriff's car park in front of the rental office. His nostrils flared up as he sucked his teeth.

"Pussy ass mutha fuckas," he said to himself, parking his car in the next set of apartments by Renee's.

Fast Blacc sat behind the tinted windows of the Buick Regal examining everything that moved. He pulled apart the panel on top of the dashboard where the air bag use to be removing a Glock 26. Leaning back in his seat he concealed the weapon in the waistband of his jeans covering it with his shirt before stepping out of the car. His curiosity and eagerness pulled his body like a powerful magnet towards Renee's apartment. Fast Blacc took precaution storing each face that cast a glance in his direction into his memory. The fine hairs stood up along the base of his neck. It was a feeling he got when he became paranoid.

The words "No Mistake No Mercy Nigga" began whispering in the back of his mind. He scanned the faces but didn't see anyone observing or shadowing him. He cut through the next set of apartments walking through the breezeway. Before he had a chance to turn around, he saw a Harris County Sheriff talking to a light brown complected female. The girl raised her hand pointing at Fast Blacc while still talking to the Sheriff.

"HEY, COME HERE!" the Sheriff yelled out, as soon as he turned around in his direction. The Sheriff reached for his revolver, but Fast Blacc was already kicking up dust before he hollered out, "FREEZE!"

A fear-fueled adrenaline rushed to his brain at the stimulus of being chased and maybe caught. Fast Blacc reached for his Glock 26 throwing two shots behind his back without looking. His actions were answered by a response from the Sheriff's 357 Smith & Wesson spitting bullets inches from his head. Fast Blacc stopped and ducked behind a parked car returning fire. Bullets tore up chunks of concrete as the Sheriff ran for cover on the side of the apartment building. The Sheriff peeked his head from around the corner, and a bullet ripped through his ear making him scream out in pain.

Fast Blacc heard the Sheriff holler out in pain and wasted no time running towards I-10. The Sheriff held his ear poking his head around the corner of the building just in time to see Fast Blacc running towards the freeway. Fast Blacc ran across the median strip and up the slope along the side of the freeway. The Sheriff was closing distance quickly while he stood there looking back. Without hesitation he jumped over the concrete barrier running along the shoulder of the freeway. The Sheriff copycatted his move with his revolver in his hand. The Sheriff took aim as he ran entertaining the thought of taking a shot at Fast Blacc.

Cars zoomed by as The Sheriff chased his suspect inching closer with each foot pounding against the pavement. Fast Blacc stopped, turned around and took a shot at the Sheriff, then dashed across I-10 West with no care for his life. He cleared the first lane without getting pulverized. A car in the second lane swerved to the right flipping over slamming into a concrete barrier. Fast Blacc raised his gun firing a shot into the windshield of a car in the third lane. The driver of the car smashed on the brakes making his car's tires scream.

The move paid off for Fast Blacc causing a domino effect of havoc. An eighteen-wheeler plowed into the back of the Geo Prism sending the car flying into the air. The eighteen-wheeler's wheels rumbled trying to stop, but to no avail the trailer of the truck jackknife. Three cars crashed into the trailer of the truck exploding upon contact. Fast Blacc cleared the last lane hopping over the next concrete barrier onto the east bound side of the freeway. He ran against the traffic down the shoulder of the freeway until he noticed the cars slowing down. Fast Blacc peered back across the westbound side peeping the scene of his own destruction.

The Sheriff was nowhere in sight. Fast Blacc turned around with the flow of the traffic. Once he found a safe place to cross the freeway, he took advantage of the opportunity. With the handle of his gun he busted out the driver's window of a Dodge Charger. The shattered glass flew in the hysterical screaming woman's face. Fast Blacc snatched her through the busted window throwing her on the ground. He jumped into the car driving down the shoulder of the freeway until reaching the first exit.

Maneuvering the car with his left hand he made a sharp right turn down Waco Street. He wiped the sweat that was raining down his face with his right forearm. Fast Blacc pulled into a corner store quickly looking around before exiting the car cautiously. He walked to the nearest Metro Bus stop waiting for the first bus to arrive. The Glock 26 pressed against his stomach, and the adrenaline pumping through him had his brain in overdrive.

The Metro Bus arrived in less than five minutes. Fast Blacc paid his fair taking a seat at the back of the bus. His heart rate began slowing back to normal. A menacing smile wormed across his face thinking about his getaway. He reached into his pocket pulling out his cell phone to call Redline. He completely forgot about the fifty-thousand dollars that was in Lyric's possession. He smiled at his mistake of leaving the money behind.

"I got your money and the situation with our little bitch is taken care of," Fast Blacc said, as soon as he heard Redline's voice. "Meet me in Haverstock apartments on Lee Road and 525. After I give you your money, me and you are through," Fast Blacc continued, before ending the call with a mischievous grin on his face.

He reached up pressing the indication strip with his index finger notifying the bus driver of his stop. Fast Blacc exited the bus a block over from Lockwood, quickly making his way over to the Lockwood Inn Motel. The owner of the motel was heavily into using drugs. When Fast Blacc found out he took advantage of the occasion paying for a whole year in advance with a couple ounces of cocaine. Once he made it inside of his room he fell straight back onto the bed staring up at the ceiling with a smile on his face.

(THOSE WHO LAUGH FIRST, DON'T ALWAYS LAUGH LAST.)

CHAPTER 54

"TIME TO DIE"
(FEDERAL ROAD)
HOUSTON, TEXAS

R edline sat on the edge of the bed with his head down. All his problems were soon to be eliminated with the death of Fast Blacc. The mind-blowing sex Hollywood served had his thoughts distracted. He glanced back at Hollywood laying sprawled across the bed on her stomach. Redline eased up from the bed and put on his clothes. Standing in front of the dresser looking at his reflection in the mirror he took a deep breath.

Ever since he was released from prison, he hadn't had the chance to sit back and enjoy himself, without being on the defensive end with Hollywood. Between plotting and scheming to cover up his tracks, and keeping a close eye on Hollywood, he needed a serious break. From the illumination of the burning candles, he saw Hollywood standing on the bed with her arms outstretch towards him. He turned around quickly with fear coursing through his body from the sight of her face. To his surprise, Hollywood was still laying across the bed in the same position. A chilling feeling fluttered over his body making him shrug his shoulders.

He turned back around staring at the mirror in disbelief at what he had seen, only to see his own reflection. Redline turn around again, as Hollywood shift her body in another position. He shook the crazy thought out of his head walking out of the bedroom. Securing the .25

automatic in the ankle strap around his left leg, he adjusted his pants to conceal the weapon. He checked the clip in his nickel plated .45 life taker. Satisfied that the clip was full, he loaded one into the chamber. Redline left out of the house with only one thing on his brain, and that was taking Fast Blacc out of this mind-numbing equation.

The air of the night was cool, with a light breeze blowing throughout the quiet subdivision. He stepped into his car and fired up a Black & Mild before turning the ignition. Redline glanced up at the house making sure Hollywood wasn't moving around. He couldn't describe the feeling he was experiencing, because when a black widow stalks its prey, she watches with keen eyes, and waits patiently until it's time to kill. He inhaled from the Black & Mild, backing his car out of the driveway ignoring the dreadful feeling.

(FATALITY MOVES IN SILENCE, AND COMES
WHEN YOU LEAST EXPECT IT.)

$$$

Inside the house, Hollywood quickly got dressed as soon as she heard the front door close. The phone call Redline received late in the night, instantly activated her vicious inner thoughts. The way Redline quietly whispered into the phone, asking the caller where to meet up at, didn't sit right with her at all. Rushing to put her pants on, she stumbled down to the floor swearing out loud. Hollywood stood to her feet pulling her pants up. She put on her shirt and shoes. Removing the .32 automatic hidden behind the mirror on the dresser, she placed it into her purse. She had a license to carry a weapon something Redline wasn't aware of.

Hollywood rushed out of the house quickly jumping into her SUV. She activated the tracking device she purchased from Spy Tech, which instantly lit up the screen on her cell phone. The red dot navigated on the screen as she watched the GPS, fresh on his trail. She reversed out of the driveway beginning her chase.

Hollywood gripped the steering wheel increasing the speed,

glancing from her smart phone back to the road. The image of Fast Blacc jump out of nowhere into her brain. An eerie feeling coursed through her mind, that Redline was on his way to meet Fast Blacc. Hollywood watched as the red dot inched its way on the screen, moving down I-10 West. She peered into the rearview mirror before merging into the right lane. Her mind was made up to kill Fast Blacc whenever she saw him.

The promise she made her brother Pee Wee to punish everyone who was involved in his death, lingered freshly in her mind. She glanced at the red dot taking US 59 North. Hollywood was less than five minutes away. She pressed her foot down harder on the gas pedal. She watched as Redline exit 525 making a left turn. Her palms were sweating from gripping the steering wheel aggressively. She wiped her hands on her pants legs. Hollywood exit the freeway making a left turn at the traffic light underneath the bridge. She noticed that the red dot halted on the screen of her smart phone.

Traveling down 525 through two traffic lights, Hollywood made a right turn into a set of apartments call Haverstock. She parked in the first available spot she saw. The red-light blipped on the screen. She glanced around looking for Redline's CTS. Hollywood remove the .32 automatic from out of her purse. She slid the slide back registering a bullet into the chamber.

Before she got out of her SUV, she saw individuals striding throughout the apartment complex on missions of their own. She glanced down at her cell phone for the time, which displayed 3:00a.m. The nightlife was in full swing. People were moving around like it was the middle of the afternoon. Hollywood got out of her SUV with the chrome .32 automatic concealed in the waistband of her jeans. The only thing she had on her mind was solving her brother's death.

(WOMEN ACT OUT FROM EMOTIONS WHICH CAN BE VERY DEADLY.)

CHAPTER 55

"NO MISTKAES NO MERCY"
(HAVERSTOCK APARTMENTS)
HOUSTON, TEXAS

Fast Blacc sat behind the steering wheel in another dope fiend rental car waiting for Redline. He slowly dragged on his third sherm anxiously anticipating his arrival. Under his left thigh hidden from view. rest a .40 Cal Desert Baby Eagle. A sealed manila envelope sat in his lap, filled with cut pieces of newspaper that he planned on using as a distraction.

Hustlers and fiends moved throughout the complex without a care of anyone watching. Fast Blacc wasn't worried about the police showing up, because Haverstock was one of the most notorious, drug infested, section 8 apartments in Houston. The only time the police showed up is when they had to, which was after someone was dead and stinking. His cell phone vibrated in his hand.

"What's up?" Fast Blacc answered.

"I'm here where are you?" Redline asked, looking at the busy activity that was going on around the apartments.

"I'm all the way in the back to your left. I'm posted up in the blue Ford Taurus," he said.

"Alright," Redline said, ending the call stepping out of his car. Redline decided to walk just in case he had to make a quick getaway. He took a different route through the apartments in order to peep Fast Blacc's location without being seen.

"What's up baby! You wanna do a lil' something with this?" a crack-head whore asked, motioning her hands over her body.

"N'all I'm good lil' momma," Redline told her.

"Are you sho? Cause baby, you don't know what you missin'," the crackhead whore said, smiling revealing a set of crooked butter-colored teeth.

Redline shook his head reaching into his pocket handing the woman a twenty-dollar bill. He just wanted to get her out of his face.

"Thank you, baby! Are you sho you don't wanna take a trip to paradise? You so cute, I won't even charge you."

Redline walked off before she had a chance to continue running her mouth. When he made it to the back of the apartments, he saw the blue Ford Taurus parked in a dark secluded area. There was no way he could sneak up on Fast Blacc without being spotted. Redline glanced around with a smirk on his face walking towards the car. He gave Fast Blacc credit at choosing his meet up spot, which was in a discreet, cutthroat vicinity.

Redline held his smile as he got closer to Fast Blacc's car. He had every intention of using Fast Blacc's illogical thinking to his advantage, not knowing they both had the same thing in mind. Redline opened the car door and got inside.

"Damn nigga, it took you long enough," Fast Blacc snapped. "Man, fuck the dumb shit! What's up?" Redline said, gritting his teeth with a scorn expression on his face.

Fast Blacc sucked at his teeth looking at Redline with full body resentment.

"The only trail leading back to that nigga Pee Wee, is me and you. Your homeboy in the hospital is a different story. I should've fucked him off when I had the chance," Fast Blacc said, with venom flowing off every word.

Just to hear Fast Blacc mention his homeboy Flagg's name, made the muscles in his jaw stand out, as he ground his teeth together.

"After today, me and you are through with each other. I handled up with everyone who knew anything about our business."

Redline absorbed every word Fast Blacc was saying. He looked around at his surroundings in search of a discreet getaway route. His hand casually wormed its way closer to the .45 that was awaiting his grip. As if reading his mind, Fast Blacc tossed the envelope filled with the cut-up pieces of newspaper on his lap.

"It's the money you gave that lil' bitch," Fast Blacc told him, reaching his hand under his thigh grabbing the .40 Cal.

Redline reached down opening the envelope. A dumbfounded look instantly etched across his face. When he looked up, his eyes were staring down the barrel of the .40 Cal Desert Baby Eagle. Fast Blacc smiled as his brows drew together into a murderous scowl. Redline's mind quickly filled with thoughts of surviving. His heart hammered with fear looking into the dark icy eyes of his enemy.

"You should've just left this bullshit alone. But no, you wanna be captain save a ho. Maybe I can fuck that fine ass bitch now, since you won't be around," Fast Blacc said, laughing at his own choice of words.

Redline wanted to take a chance and reach for the .45 resting in his waistband, but the look of death in Fast Blacc's eyes changed his mind. Before Redline's selection of words were able to depart from his mouth, a dark shadow cascade over the interior of the car. Fast Blacc slightly turned his head facing the driver's window. His mouth dropped open gaping at what he saw. Before he even had a chance to turn his head back towards Redline, a bullet shattered the window puncturing through his brain, sending mist of blood spraying throughout the car. Fast Blacc's index finger involuntarily contracted squeezing the trigger. A thunderous sound roared through the night. The bullet graze Redline across his back.

Hollywood stood on the outside of the car emptying the clip into Fast Blacc's face. Her finger continued pulling the trigger well after the gun was empty. Redline looked into her dark eyes flashing with menace. But, just as quickly as he saw it, it disappeared. A mischievous smile crooked at the corners of her mouth. Redline felt her eyes gazing. The image of Hollywood laying across the bed when he left home cross his mind.

"You thought I was at home huh?'" Hollywood asked, giving him a look that paralyzed his tongue.

Goosebumps tingle up his arms when Hollywood voiced his thoughts out loud.

"Let's get the fuck outta here before the laws come," Redline told her, avoiding the question.

Hollywood could feel her cheek twitching holding back her smile. Her face heated at the thought of Redline's betrayal. Her spiteful thoughts were momentarily erased at the sight of blood soaking through his shirt. Her eyes gripped him in her dark stare, as the caring in her voice cut through their quietness.

"Baby are you alright?"

"Yeah! We just need to get outta here," Redline said, as the burning sensation sent a jolt of pain to his brain. He felt the blood running down his back. His mind began thinking that the gunshot wound was worse than it really was.

"Can you drive?" Hollywood asked, not wanting to leave his side during his time of need.

"I'm cool, just follow me home," he said, getting into his car.

Hollywood ran to her SUV jumping inside. She followed behind him as he drove by. Mixed emotions stretched her thoughts in different directions between love and betrayal. The love she had for Redline clouded her mind. Hollywood sped down the freeway trying to keep up with him. She zipped in and out of lanes with Redline on her mind, mainly the deceitful ways he had betrayed her trust.

(DECEIT, BETRAYAL, DISHONER, LIES, MISTRUST, CAN ALL LEAD TO DEATH FROM THE HANDS OF A LOVER.)

CHAPTER 56

"CONTEMPLATING"
(THE RITZ CABARET)
HOUSTON, TEXAS

After Tron left Kelly Court apartments, instead of riding around in circles he took 1-45 South heading towards The Ritz Cabaret. His mind continued pondering the whereabouts of Lil' Branon and Renee. Rubbing a hand across his face he blew air through his lips. He glanced around the parking lot noticing his aunt Diane's car wasn't there. Tron hopped out of his car and was greeted by the bouncer known as Big Thay, who faithfully worked the door without missing a day.

Big Thay gave Tron a pound with a fist that felt more like a sledgehammer than a human hand. Tron went straight to his aunt's office to relax his mind and sort through his options at locating Fast Blacc. No one was home when he stopped at Lyric's girlfriend's apartment in Greenspoint. Tron didn't have a number to call Lyric, so he had no choice but to wait and see if she would call him. He poured himself a stiff drink of Don Julio 70, filling the glass halfway. He took a sip that burned all the way down to his stomach. Reaching for an ashtray, Tron sat down lighting a Black & Mild.

Peering through the two-way backdrop of the wall size fish tank, he saw a dancer working herself slowly and seductively against a pole. She had her head leaned back, lost in her own images in her mind. Tron instantly thought about the night he was with Lyric and Naliah. He wondered what would have transpired if Lyric hadn't received that call from Fast Blacc. He took a drag from the Black & Mild before sipping his drink. Tron went through the contacts on his iPhone locating Redline's number. Redline was the only source he had left at finding Fast Blacc. The line rang as he peered at a pair of convict fish fighting each other.

"Yeah!" Redline answered, knowing the area code but not the number.

"What's up pimp?" Tron asked, staring at the dancer holding the pole with both hands dropping to the ground with her legs spread.

"Man, who the fuck is this?"

"It's Tron nigga! If you're busy, I'll hit you back up later."

"N'all man, my bad. I just been through too much shit for one day," Redline said, feeling Hollywood's eyes boring in the back of his head.

"I was just hittin' you up tryin' to see if you heard anything about Fast Blacc?" Tron contemplated the silence over the phone before talking again. "Say my nigga, if it's a bad time hit me back when you can talk." Redline reached for the remote control stealing a glance in Hollywood's direction to see if she was paying him any attention.

"You don't have to worry about that nigga no more. You feel me? I'll run things down to you when I get back from the hospital. Me and my gal are finna go visit my homeboy Flagg," Redline told him.

"I can read between the lines. That's all I need to hear. Fuck with me whenever you can, cause we need to talk about that connect," Tron said, raising his eyebrows.

"Bet that!" Redline said, ending the call.

Tron sat there with a slow smile spreading across his face. He took a deep drag from the Black & Mild finishing the remainder of his drink before exhaling. Since Fast Blacc was dead, Tron knew Lyric was nowhere alive. Ralo skipped across his mind, because of the dumb move that could have ruined his plans before they were set into motion. He smiled at the thought of Pee Wee being easily mislead. Tron began laughing to himself, stepping out of the office in search of Naliah. He knew once he had Redline's connect, there was no stopping him from rising to the top. And once he had a chance at making some real money—Redline was history.

(FOR THE LOVE OF MONEY, MOST WILL KILL THEIR OWN BROTHERS.)

CHAPTER 57

"DISHONEST LOVER"
(BEN TAUB HOSPITAL)
HOUSTON, TEXAS

Hollywood and Redline were heading to the hospital to visit his homeboy Flagg. She tried to get Redline to go and see a doctor about his wound. Redline refused to take any chances with his freedom by making silly mistakes, like going to a hospital about a bullet wound. He knew the police would be the first ones notified, therefore he settled for the next best thing. He had Hollywood treat his gunshot wound. Since their run in with Fast Blacc their conversation had been held to a minimum.

Hollywood was entombed in her own cunning ideas for a farewell departure of her dishonest lover. A forceful smile appeared on her face as she reached over holding his hand. Redline sat in his seat sideways avoiding direct pressure on his wound. He felt the moisture of his hand holding Hollywood's. Nervousness became an issue whenever he visited Flagg. He didn't like looking at his homeboy laying in a hospital bed when he knew he was the one to blame. An image of Hollywood danced around in his mind as she unloaded the clip into Fast Blacc's body.

The sight of her face sent a hair-raising chill through his body. "We're here baby!" Hollywood said, squeezing his hand jolting him out of his trance.

Redline gazed into her eyes looking for any hint of perception to his deceitfulness. Hollywood cast a deceptive smile in his direction before getting out of the SUV. Redline shrugged his shoulders trying his best to shake away the uneasy feeling he was experiencing. The words, "SHE KNOWS I DID IT," kept running through his conscience. He shook the warning out of his head walking towards the hospital with Hollywood by his side.

The electric sliding doors parted as they walk into the entrance. Ben Taub Hospital was busy with activity as usual. The waiting area was filled to capacity with people standing and sitting on the floor. Hollywood shook her head at the sight proceeding towards the elevator. Redline pressed the arrow pointing up for the elevator, trying to ward off the uneasy feeling of being in the hospital where Flagg was at. The elevator was packed as they squeezed their way inside. Hollywood stood behind Redline with her arms around his waist. Even though he committed the worst betrayal within their relationship, Hollywood's love was until the end.

The elevator doors opened, and they stepped off walking towards Flagg's room hand in hand. A feeling of guilt fell over him as soon as he pushed the door open. Redline felt like he betrayed Flagg, even though he didn't know Flagg was in the car before Pee Wee was killed. Hollywood sat in a chair by the window. Her gaze was on Redline standing by Flagg's bedside. He stood looking down at his homeboy feeling remorseful, while Hollywood stared at him remorselessly. Hollywood knew Redline had a weakness when it came to his homeboy Flagg, so their visit to the hospital was premeditated on her behalf.

Hollywood had her own plans, and they started with studying her surroundings. Vindictiveness quivered through her veins increasing her heart rate. A sly smile began forming on her face. She stood up walking next to Redline. Her eyes gripped him in her dark gaze. The passion in her voice cut through the quietness. "Baby, I know how you feel for Flagg. And I also know how you love him like he's your own brother. But you have to stay strong for him. If your heart is real, GOD will answer your prayers," Hollywood said, standing up on her tip toes placing a tender kiss on his cheek.

Redline swallowed his guilt quickly batting away his tears before they fell. Hollywood glanced uneasily at the tubes and wires connected to the equipment. Redline reached down shaking Flagg's hand before they left the room. The weight of regret disappeared as soon as he started walking down the hallway. Hollywood looked in his direction as he inhaled a deep breath sighing. They rode the elevator back down in silence lost in their own thoughts. They both had secrets they were keeping from each other. However, Hollywood knew the secret Redline was planning on taking to the grave. She drove home with her black widow thoughts weaving a web for her prey.

(A WOMAN IS VERY PATIENT. BUT WHEN HER PATIENCE RUNS OUT, SHE CAN BE VERY DEADLY.)

CHAPTER 58

"REAP WHAT YOU SOW"
(FEDERAL ROAD)
HOUSTON, TEXAS

Hollywood bathed Redline, carefully washing around the gunshot wound that stretch across his back. The sight of the long deep gash made her flesh crawl. Hollywood shrug the feeling away. Despite his misleading relentless ways, she still cared for him with all her heart. She dried him off, trying her best not to pay attention to his dick throbbing in her hand. Merely inches away from her mouth, Hollywood couldn't control the temptation that was beckoning her skillful and willing tongue.

She wrapped her hand around the base of his dick placing the head into her mouth. Redline reach down and put his hand on the back of her head. Hollywood instantly stopped. Communicating only with her eyes, Redline removed his hand from the back of her head. Hollywood smiled and went right back to work. She stroked his dick slowly working her way further down its length. She coated his dick with saliva working her hand and neck at the same time. Redline moaned out in pleasure reaching for her head again. He caught himself, quickly jerking his hand back. Hollywood deep throated his dick with spit running down the corners of her mouth. His knees began to buckle as she increased her suction and hand motion. His hands slid down the wall sitting down on the edge of the bathtub. Hollywood rested her hands on the floor and worked her neck in his lap as if she had an attitude.

Redline spread his legs wider, thrusting his hips forward with his right hand resting inside of the bathtub. Hollywood felt his body shake, as his dick began swelling in her mouth. She knew he was about to cum. She eased up to the tip of his dick sucking vigorously. He grunted loudly, shooting his seed into her mouth, stretching his legs as his toes began curling. Hollywood sucked every drop before rinsing her mouth with mouthwash, then brushing her teeth.

Redline sat on the floor with his back against the bathtub watching her every move. When she finished, Hollywood left the bathroom looking back over her shoulder. He sat slouching on the floor with the back of his head resting on the edge of the bathtub, with a satisfying look on his face. Hollywood smiled, walking into the kitchen to finish preparing their meal. She glanced down at her watch noticing it was 7:00 p.m.

She had less than three hours to follow through with her plan and make it back home. Hollywood peeped over her shoulder as Redline was walking into the kitchen. He put his arms around her waist, kissing her on the neck as she stood in front of the stove. The smell of salmon, mixed with extra virgin olive oil, sautéed in onions and garlic, attack his nostrils. Hollywood closed her eyes enjoying the warmth and the hardness of his body.

The salmon sizzling in the pan, mingling with the aroma of wild rice, green beans with butter, and oven baked dinner rolls, topped with cinnamon sweet butter float throughout the air. Hollywood felt Redline becoming aroused grinding against her backside. She playfully swatted his hands away from her waist. If she wanted to carry out her plans, she had to be strong, and not fall weak over a good piece of dick.

Hollywood fixed their plates. She piled his plate with food knowing he would eat every bit. And after his stomach was full, he would relax on the couch and quickly fall asleep. One thing Hollywood knew, and knew quite well, was her man. She smiled as he devoured his meal with a smirk on his face. When they finished, Hollywood did the dishes at a slow pace, allowing Redline time for his food to digest, and to get comfortable.

Hollywood walked into the bathroom to grab some medical tape, bandages, and ointment to dress his wound. Redline was laid across the couch on his stomach, fighting to keep his eyes open watching television. Hollywood gently applied the ointment and dressings to his wound without saying a word. He lay there lost in his own thoughts, drifting closer to sleep. Hollywood called his name to see if he was sleeping. When she didn't get a response, she grabbed her purse and headed straight out the door. Glancing down at her watch she saw it was 8:45 p.m.

She had less than an hour and fifteen minutes to handle her business and make it back home. Hollywood jumped in her SUV riding off into the night. She was on a serious mission. One step closer to ending her problems.

(I AIN'T A KILLER BUT DON'T PUSH ME!)

CHAPTER 59

"REVENGE IS A BITCH"
(BEN TAUB HOSPITAL)
HOUSTON, TEXAS

Hollywood, casually stepping off an elevator disguised in a red wig and a pair of dark sunglasses. Her eyes darted up and down the hallway before entering the hospital room. She checked the restroom first, remembering how she startled Amber when she first met her. Hollywood didn't have time for any dumb mistakes on her behalf. She walked over to Flagg's bedside as an odd feeling shot over her body. She turned around at the feeling of being watched. Her mind was playing tricks for the wrongful deed she was about to commit. She looked down at Flagg and froze with an appalled expression on her face.

Flagg lay there staring right into her eyes. Hollywood's heart began hammering with fear of being caught in the act. Flagg's eyes bore into hers, wondering what the hell was she doing. He didn't recognize the girl behind the dark sunglasses and red wig. Flagg was paralyzed from the neck down, with tubes running through his mouth and nostrils. Hollywood felt her tears running down her face. She had nothing against Flagg, but the love Redline displayed for him was a sign of weakness she had to capitalize on.

Hollywood reached for the pillow as Flagg stared into her eyes. Tears cascade down his cheeks as he came to realize what was about to happen. His eyes screamed "WHY?" as they became bigger the closer the pillow got to his face. Hollywood was in mid motion of stopping, but she forced herself to follow through with vengeance for her brother's death. She smashed the pillow forcefully down on Flagg's face. His head struggled side to side. Hollywood pressed the pillow harder until his movement ceased. She looked around again experiencing a freakish feeling of someone watching her.

Without removing the pillow away from his face, she snatched all the tubes from the monitors and equipment. A soft, low beep began humming when she kicked the plug out of the electrical socket. Wasting not a second more, Hollywood quickly walk out the door. Her heart pounded dully in her ears as her eyes zip in both directions, down the hallway. Taking the stairs back down to the first floor, one of her heels broke off her shoe. Hollywood reached down pulling both of her shoes off her feet.

With her shoes in her left hand, she held the handrail taking each step as quickly as possible. Once she reached the lower level, she slowed her stride. Hollywood walked through the lobby discreetly, not drawing any unwanted attention to her escape. She exited the hospital, walking two blocks over jumping inside of her SUV. A feeling of relief overcame her body as soon as she turned the ignition. The image of Flagg's face jumped out in her mind. His eyes stared at her in desperation for his life. The eerie feeling of being watched stuck with her, it made the hairs on the back of her neck stand at attention. Hollywood ignored the warning heading back home to complete her unfinished business. A smile snaked across her face at the thought of fulfilling the promise she gave her brother after his death.

(SOME SAY PROMISES ARE MEANT TO BE BROKEN. BUT WHEN UNCONDITIONAL LOVE IS INVOLVED, THERE ARE NO EXCUSES.)

CHAPTER 60

"KARMA CALLS"
(FEDERAL ROAD)
HOUSTON, TEXAS

The constant ringing of a telephone continued to drone within Redline's mind. He finally woke up and realize the phone was ringing in the house. He got up instantly feeling the wetness on the front of his shorts. He shook his head as he remembered the wet dream.

"Yeah!" he said, answering the phone.

"This is Dr. Wilson here at Ben Taub General Hospital. This number was listed just in case of an emergency." Redline knew the next words were about to be bad news. "Wilbert Hunter was found dead," Dr. Wilson continued.

Redline didn't understand anything she said after he heard "FOUND DEAD."

"Hello! Hello, are you still there?" Redline stood holding the phone with a dumbfound look on his face.

$$$

Hollywood threw the red wig and sunglasses into a dumpster on her way home. She glanced down at her watch pulling into her driveway. She was surprised she made it back home before 10 o'clock. She wondered if Redline was still sleeping. Hollywood heard the telephone ringing walking up to the front door. A curious look crossed her face as she wondered who was calling her home phone.

The phone rang again before she opened the door. Hollywood stepped into the house and saw Redline standing like a statue. He was holding the telephone down by his side. A disturbing look was engraved on his face as tears slide down his face. She knew the call came from the hospital about Flagg. The sight of him standing in an emotional state of shock had her smiling on the insides. Redline look up into her eyes. Instantly, her happy feelings turned into sadness at witnessing the love of her life staring back at her hurting. Her emotions were in a pandemonium and she couldn't control herself. She hugged him, sharing his pain with tears of her own.

"What's wrong baby? Is everything alright?" Hollywood asked, knowing the answer she was about to receive. She tried her best to keep her feelings in check, because her weak emotions would only delay the task at hand.

"That was—Dr. Wilson. She said Flagg was found dead this morn-ing," Redline said, slowly and incoherently.

"What else did she say?" Hollywood asked, wondering if anyone saw her coming are going. When Redline didn't answer she reach for the phone. Dr. Wilson explained to Hollywood all that she knew, which was very little. Her heart dropped into the bottom of her stomach when Dr. Wilson told her the police were investigating and reviewing the cameras.

Hollywood thanked her before hanging up the phone. "How could I be so stupid?" she thought to herself, for not realizing there were cameras, at the hospital. The more she thought about it the less worried she became.

Hollywood knew her path to revenge was coming to an end. Redline was in the bathroom sitting on the toilet with his face buried in his hands. Hollywood walked in and turned on the shower. She removed her clothes and stood in front-of him naked. Redline didn't even glance up until he heard the shower curtain sliding back. Catching a glimpse of Hollywood's firm ass cheeks stepping into the shower, placed his thoughts on a totally different page. She knew how to snatch his mind away from his problems.

Redline watching her silhouette through the shower curtain instantly becoming aroused. He stood up removing his shorts stepping into the shower. Hollywood smiled with her back facing him. She loved when a plan came together as she orchestrated it. She turned around not saying a word that would ruin the moment before it started. Hollywood turned him around slowly peeling away his bandages. After turning him back around she darted her tongue into his mouth, before he had a chance to say anything.

Hollywood applied Dove soap to a washcloth handing it to him. She felt his dick tapping against her stomach seeking attention. Redline bathed her body with finesse, staring at her with appreciation. His dick throbbed when he saw the sight of her flesh glistening under the cascade of water. Hollywood bent over, looking back seductively.

"I think you missed a spot," she told him, biting down on her bottom lip.

Redline wasted no time diving his tongue into her wetness. Hollywood moaned out in pleasure. Redline's tongue was exploring her pussy as the hot water ran between her ass cheeks. She placed her hands on her knees and worked her pussy up and down against his tongue. Hollywood gasped out when she felt his finger penetrating her asshole. Her muscles involuntarily contract tightly around his thumb and tongue. Relaxing, she placed both of her hands on the edge of the bathtub enjoying the feeling of gratification. The deeper his tongue buried itself into her ass hole, the wetter her pussy became.

Hollywood erupted as she spread her ass backing it against his face. Redline lightly toyed around with the soft flesh of her rectum. She moaned upon contact of his hot tongue. Not being able to withstand the pleasure, Hollywood stepped out of the shower. Redline had a grin on his face as he washed himself off. Hollywood grabbed a terry cloth towel walking into the bedroom.

She had to stay focused without getting sidetracked behind some good sex. Her pussy and asshole tingled from his deceitful and skillful tongue. She took a deep breath collecting her thoughts. "TILL DEATH DO US PART," were the words that motivated her villainous thoughts. A grim smile spread across her face as she dried herself off standing in front of the dresser. Hollywood looked at her reflection in the mirror, wondering why a man would betray such a beautiful and loyal woman?

The question picked at her brain making her boil with anger. The reflection staring back at her was someone she didn't recognize. They say every person has an evil alter ego, and Hollywood was meeting hers for the very first time. After drying herself off she dropped the towel on the floor walking into the kitchen. She had to grab a few essentials to carry out her devious plan.

(A PLAN WELL THOUGHT OUT CAN EASILY GO WRONG, ESPECIALLY WHEN YOU'RE BLINDED BY LOVE.)

CHAPTER 61

"RELENTLESS WAYS"
(SUPER 8 MOTEL ON AIRPORT)
HOUSTON, TEXAS

Tron and Naliah sexed each other every which way imaginable, making up for the night Lyric ruined. Naliah lay spread eagle across the bed naked with a smile on her face. She was covered with sweat. Tron blazed up a grape cigarillo filled with pineapple kush. The sex with Naliah was a good stress reliever, but his mind was stuck on Redline hooking him up with his connection.

Tron dragged slowly on the cigarillo with his mind racing with thoughts of stacking paper. He glanced at Naliah exhaling smoke through his nostrils. He couldn't understand how a female so beautiful and flawless could lower her standards sliding up and down a stripper's pole, instead of manipulating the weak-minded with her beauty. Tron shook his head at the thought, reaching for his cell phone walking outside of the room.

The cool breeze of the night blew across his body. He dialed Redline's number waiting for an answer. Hollywood's brother Pee Wee popped up in his thoughts. Tron shook his head thinking about how he should have gone about his scheme differently.

"Yeah, what's up?" Redline answered, sounding annoyed.

Tron picked up on his attitude but smartly held his composure. "Say pimp! I don't wanna keep sweatin' you. But I got so many licks and they keep blowin' my phone up. You feel me?" Tron heard Redline laughing.

"My bad my nigga! I just forgot to hit you back up. I talked to my connect and everything is jumpin' off tomorrow. He wants you to meet him at Magic Island off of 59 at twelve o'clock. Tell the hostess your name and everything else is set," Redline explained.

Tron was filled with stimulus when he heard the good news that would change his lifestyle for the best.

"Man, good lookin' out pimp. I owe you one," Tron said, with one hand on the balcony rail looking at the cars driving down Airport Blvd.

"Just don't let me down man," Redline told him.

"Don't worry about it, I got you," Tron said, with a smirk on his face.

"I'll holla at you later," Redline said, ending the call.

Tron walked back inside the room firing back up the cigarillo he left in the ashtray. As he inhaled the kush, his mind flashed back to the day him and Pee Wee had a conversation...Hollywood's brother.

"Look out pimp! I don't know why you keep paying Redline all that money every month. You're the one out here takin' all the penitentiary chances." Pee Wee noddeded his head in agreement to what Tron was saying. "It's like he's pimpin' you instead of helpin' you. What type of brother-n-law is that?" Tron questioned, looking at him hoping the seed of greed would take root and sprout.

"Man, come to think about it. You're-goddamn right. I'm the one out here moving this work faster than the speed limit," Pee Wee said.

Tron added a little bit of water to the seed of greed he planted within Pee Wee's mind.

"Plus, it ain't like he can reach you from behind bars anyway. man fuck that nigga! You been paying him ten-thousand dollars a month for two years now," Tron said, noticing the grim look that was etched on Pee Wee's face.

"Say Tron, you're right my nigga. I just never peeped it like that. After today, it's all about me. Fuck that ho ass nigga," Pee wee told him, with a scowl on his face exposing the platinum and diamonds in his mouth.

Tron smiled at the thought of a plan well put together. He took the last hit of the kush and snuffed the butt into the ashtray. He looked over at Naliah who was still sleeping. Tron removed his pants and jumped back into bed for another round.

(CROOKED WAYS WILL CATCH UP WITH YOU IN DUE TIME, SO BE PREPARED.)

CHAPTER 62

"DEJA VU"
(FEDERAL ROAD)
HOUSTON, TEXAS

Redline was in the shower when Hollywood walked in handing him his cell phone. He glanced at her suspiciously as she walked back out of the bathroom with her ass jiggling. He handled his business over the phone with Tron. Redline knew Tron was a hustler by heart, hungry for an opportunity to make major paper. However, the thought of betrayal crossed his mind because of the crossroad Pee Wee placed him in. Redline shook the thought out of his brain, quickly smiling at the image of Hollywood's flawless figure.

His dick stood at attention leading the way towards the bedroom. The smell of jasmine attacked his nostrils before reaching the bedroom. Candles were flickering throughout the room as the moon highlighted through the curtains. Red rose petals were scattered on top of the white satin sheets. Hollywood sat on the edge of the bed with her legs crossed, leaning back on her arms. Her eyes gleamed seduction as her mind churned revenge. Redline noticed the tray of toys and goodies sitting on the bed next to her.

A smile spread across his face as his mind anticipate the freaky activities Hollywood had in store.

"Why are you smiling like that?" Hollywood asked, biting down on her lip staring at his dick.

"Because I know how you go all out when you're feelin' yourself," Redline said, stepping right in front of her placing his hands on his hips.

"'So, you know me like a book," Hollywood told him, sitting straight up.

"Not like a book. But as the woman that stayed down with me, when no one else would. Baby, I know things been fucked up since I been out. But I want you to know I love you with all my heart," Hollywood swallowed the lump that was forming in her throat.

She tried her best to blink away the tears in her eyes before they raced down her cheeks. She never doubted the love Redline had for her. It was only his betrayal at having her brother killed that set off her rage from within. "I love you too Adrian. Till Death Do Us Apart!" Hollywood said, standing to her feet passionately kissing the man she loved with all her heart. She stepped back on top of the bed and face him. "Come here and turn around!"

Redline followed orders turning his back towards her. Hollywood reached down and grabbed two strips of satin cloth, placing one of them over his eyes. Redline smiled as the smooth material cover his eyes in total darkness.

"Open your mouth," Hollywood instructed, holding the other satin cloth in her hands.

Redline obeyed her dominatrix command. Hollywood secured the strip of cloth in his mouth tying it behind him head. She pulled him back towards the bed commanding him to sit down with his back against the headboard. Hollywood reached down snatching two pairs of handcuffs out of the tray. She placed the first pair around his left wrist and fasten the other end onto the solid oak headboard. Hollywood gently held his right hand raising it to her mouth. She slowly sucked on his index finger while stroking his dick. Redline moaned out sounds of pleasure which were muffle by the gag.

She handcuffed his right wrist clamping the other end tightly onto the headboard. Redline waited impatiently as his mind anticipated the pleasures that would take him to ecstasy. Hollywood straddled him slowly easing down on top of his dick. She gasped out as his member fill her insides. The warmth from her womb and the experience of being blindfolded, gagged, and handcuffed, had his mind far away from any potential dangers. Hollywood increased her rhythm grabbing a hold of the headboard with both hands. Both of their moans bounced off the walls as the smell of sex and jasmine waft throughout the room.

A grim look appeared on Hollywood's face as she started grinding aggressively up and down, slamming herself into his lap. The sound of her ass slapping against his thighs, mimicked the tone of loud hand clapping. Redline bit down on the gag when Hollywood's pussy muscles clamp around his dick. She felt her orgasm building up.

"Oh Adrain! Adrain! Adrain, I'm cuming!" Hollywood yelled out, climaxing.

Redline felt her juices oozing down the length of his dick to the crack of his ass. He felt himself about to erupt. Hollywood noticed he was about to cum. She raised herself up. His dick was pointing straight up at the ceiling. Hollywood reached over to the tray filled with necessities grabbing the Oneida butcher knife from underneath the towel. She turned back around stroking his dick in her left hand. Hollywood looked at him with a disgusting look on her face.

Redline moaned as she worked her hand up and down his dick. In one quick fluid motion, Hollywood swung the butcher knife completely dismembering his dick from his body. The veins and arteries that carried blood from his heart began squirting red liquid in her face. Blood streamed out as Redline screamed in agonizing pain. Hollywood wiped the blood that was running down her face with her forearm. Redline kicked and twisted uncontrollably as the handcuffs held him secure to the headboard.

His screams were muffled making him sound inhuman. Hollywood glanced at his severed body part in her left hand. Her eyes were wide open filled with a vortex of murder and hate. She licked the semen that trickled down her hand smiling crookedly. Redline's body jerked around as his veins fluctuated gushing blood each time his heartbeat. The white satin sheets were covered with streaks of blood. Redline continued his worthless struggle.

Hollywood straddled his body as he bucked underneath her. She held the butcher knife in her right hand. In her left hand she had a death grip on his cut off dick. The more Redline tried to fashion an escape, the faster his blood exit through his sliced arteries. Hollywood drove the butcher knife through the pillow, deep into the mattress. Reaching behind the headboard snatching her second gun from another Velcro strip. She looked down as Redline's tussling rage subsided.

Hollywood raised up the blindfold with the barrel of the gun. Redline looked at her with eyes filled with pain and mortification. He didn't recognize the horrific look she had engraved on her face.

"Why did you have my brother killed?" that question alone confirmed quickly in his brain that he was about to die. "I heard you and Lyric over the phone. Redline, how could you do this to me?" Hollywood asked, snatching the gag free from his mouth. "I gave you my all since the first day we met. Why? Why did you fuckin' do it?" Hollywood pushed the chrome plated .38 special against his eye socket.

Redline swallowed the fear in his throat.

"All I can say is I'm sorry—and I love you." His voice was barely above a whisper. "Those twenty books you gave your brother—he never paid me," Redline felt himself clinging desperately to life.

"Why didn't you tell me?" Hollywood yelled, pulling back the hammer on the Charles Bronson, (38 SPECIAL). Tears flowed as she threw his shriveled-up dick in his face. "Stupid mutha fucka! You could've told me that," she hollered out, grabbing the gun with both hands.

Redline strained while raising his head peering into her eyes. "I was raised by the streets—and you—!" Redline fought against the violent pain bleeding closer to death. "You know how I am about my money. And you know—how I feel about you. I'm sorry," Redline said, ready to accept his consequences.

Hollywood lowered the gun away from his face.

"You know how I feel for you. And you know my love is based on trust and honesty. I know you love me. I also know you trust me. But one thing I do know, you haven't been honest," she said, wiping her tears with the back of her hand. "But I have!"

Hollywood opened the cylinder shaking the bullets out of their chambers. Redline gazed at the bullets as they fell in his bloody lap. Hollywood reached down picking up a bullet from the puddle of blood. She stared at the blood coated bullet before placing it back into a chamber.

"I loved my brother like I love myself. I loved him like I love you," Hollywood said, spinning the revolving cylinder closing her eyes.

Redline peered on with the little life that was left in his body. She closed the cylinder locking it into place. Hollywood pulled back the hammer once again, but this time with the intent to kill.

"Since I love you so much, I'm gonna let you live. That way you can really see how much I truly love you. Till death do us part!" Hollywood said, raising the .38 special pressing it against her temple.

She closed her eyes while squeezing the trigger. CLICK...

Redline's body twitched. She opened her eyes aiming the gun against his left temple. Without hesitation she pulled the trigger. CLICK...

Redline flinched at the sound of the hammer slamming against the firing pin. His life was slipping away by the second as his blood drain from his body.

Hollywood raised the revolver back to her temple. CLICK...

Redline closed his eyes reciting the Lord's prayer before the inevitable happened.

"Forgive me for my sins LORD! And most of all—please forgive her,"

Hollywood lifted the gun back to his temple. Tears filled with love, frustration, anger, and confusion rain down her face. Redline felt the gun tremble against the flatten space on the side of his forehead. CLICK...

Hollywood leaned down kissing him on his lips. She mouthed

"I LOVE YOU," inching the hammer back. Her hand shook uncontrollably, and her finger slowly began pulling the trigger. BOOM!!!

A magnificent blood-fan imprinted an abstract expressionism on the wall. Hollywood fell right beside him displaying the grotesque testimony of her love. Redline hung from the headboard drifting closer to death's peaceful nowhere. A dull pounding sound drift from a distance. His vision was blurry as he saw several figures rushing towards him. Distorted voices were heard throughout the bedroom before he fell unconscious.

(LIFE TEACHES US ALL VALUABLE LESSONS...AND THE MOST IMPORTANT TOPIC...IS LOVE.)

CHAPTER 63

"DOUBLE CROSSED"
(SUPER 8 MOTEL ON AIRPORT)
HOUSTON, TEXAS

Tron sat on the edge of the bed removing tobacco from a Philly Blunt. Naliah was in the shower washing away their night of hot sex. He turned on the television flipping through the channels, stopping on the news. Tron skillfully began rolling the pineapple kush tightly into the Blunt paper. He kicked his feet back up on the bed and enjoyed his blunt, watching the Channel 2 News. The Pineapple taste filled his lungs. He heard Naliah singing in the shower, thinking she needed to stick with the stripping, and leave the singing to the professionals. Tron smiled at the thought, exhaling through his nostrils. He turned up the news broadcast drowning out Naliah's horrible singing.

"GOOD MORNING TO THOSE WHO ARE JUST WAKING UP. HOWEVER, IT WASN'T REALLY A GOOD MORNING FOR A COUPLE THAT STAYED HERE, OFF OF FEDERAL ROAD ON THE EASTSIDE OF HOUSTON. MERELY AN HOUR AGO, NEIGHBORS HEARD SCREAMING VOICES COMING FROM WITHIN THIS RESIDENCE BEHIND ME. DESCRIBED AS A LOVING OUIET COUPLE FROM ONE NEIGHBOR, AN ELDERLY WOMAN WHO HAS BEEN STAYING HERE FOR OVER TWENTY YEARS."

"I JUST WOKE UP TO FIX MY HUSBAND SOME COFFEE,

LIKE I DO EVERY MORNING. THAT WAS WHEN I HEARD LOUD SCREAMING. I THOUGHT MY MIND WAS PLAYING WITH ME. BECAUSE YOU KNOW HOW YOUR HEARING GETS WHEN YOU'RE MY AGE. I WALKED INTO OUR BACK-YARD AND HEARD THE SCREAMING COMING FROM NEXT DOOR. THE WAY IT SOUNDED, I JUST HAD TO CALL 911." The elder woman explained.

"THAT 911 CALL MAY HAVE SAVED THE LIFE OF ADRAIN JONES. HE WAS FOUND HANDCUFFED TO THEIR HEAD-BOARD SECONDS AWAY FROM DEATH. HE WAS BLEEDING PROFUSELY FROM BEING CASTRATED. YES, ANOTHER HAIR-RAISING SCENE-SIMILAR TO LORENA AND JOHN WAYNE BOBBIT."

Tron grabbed his crotch area cringing at the thought of having his dick cut off. He inhaled the kush shaking his head at what he was hearing.

"BUT THIS SCENE DIDN'T TURN OUT GOOD. THE WOMAN WHO WAS IDENTIFIED AS DYCHELLE JONES, COMMITTED SUICIDE BY SHOOTING HERSELF IN THE HEAD. SHE WAS FOUND DEAD LAYING ACROSS HER HUSBAND AS HE BLED SECONDS AWAY FROM DEATH. AS FOR WHETHER THE VICTIM SURVIVED, WE ARE UNABLE TO DETERMINE AT THIS PARTICULAR TIME. WHEN ANY FURTHER INFORMATION COMES UP YOU WILL BE UPDATED. THIS IS TIARA MOUTON, REPORTING LIVE FOR CHANNEL 2 NEWS."

Tron sat there lost in his own daze as the kush burn slowly. "You see what happen when you niggas play with a woman's emotions," Naliah said, walking out of the bathroom catching the end of the broadcast.

Tron thought about what she said inhaling the potent weed. He watched as Naliah was putting on her clothes, thinking about the dude who got his dick cut off. He didn't realize he knew Adrain Jones. Majority of street hustlers never went by their birth given names, only a select few. And Tron was one of them. Grabbing his watch from the nightstand he peeped the time. Tron saw he had less than four hours to kill before his twelve o'clock rendezvous with Redline's connection.

He glanced at Naliah wiggling her assets into her jeans. The kush had him feeling good. Tron was hoping the rest of the day would turn out even better. He took another hit from the blunt passing it to Naliah. For some strange reason he couldn't keep his mind off of the dude getting his dick chopped off. Tron took a steaming hot shower and got himself ready for the day that lay ahead.

After dropping Naliah off at her apartment in Broadway Square, he drove to Sharpstown mall. He walked around the mall for thirty minutes before deciding on a purchase. He went back to the motel room, put on his clothes heading right back out the door. Tron made a quick detour stopping at High Quality barbershop, for a fresh taper fade and a Steve Harvey edge up. He was a firm believer at making a good first impression, and his appearance was on top of the list.

Twin had him in and out of the barber's chair in less than ten minutes. Tron stood up admiring his reflection in the mirror. He grabbed a small hand mirror from off the counter to look at the back of his head. An uneven smile began forming at the edges of his mouth. Tron paid Twin for his services and took a second look at himself before leaving. The last thing he had to do was get his brain right before twelve o'clock.

Tron drove down Scott street heading towards the Trey (THIRD WARD). He made a prompt stop on MacGowen and Scott, scooping up a zone of Burberry kush from Coop, the owner of Underworld Entertainment. He zipped in and out without any small talk. He made another stop at a corner store on Alabama and Delano, snatching up a pack of strawberry blunts. Tron sliced through a blunt with a brand-new Pal (RAZOR BLADE) emptying out the tobacco. He filled the blunt with kush peeping his surroundings. After twisting and firing up the blunt he drove off.

Tron checked the time on his watch blending into traffic. He made it to Magic Island fifteen minutes ahead of time. The valet parked his car upon arrival. He walked inside of the restaurant feeling good, looking good, and smelling good. The hostess greeted him with hospitality before asking him his name. "My name is Tron," he answered.

"Oh! We have been expecting you Mr. Tron. Will you follow me please," the hostess replied, making her way through the restaurant.

The atmosphere was laid back with dim lighting. The conversations from other patrons were held to a low murmur. Tron glanced down at the hostess' ass in her skintight uniform. He licked his lips at the sight, imagining what her body would look like naked. A magician was on the center stage performing his skill mystic. The crowd clapped at his mind-boggling antics. The hostess glided through the dining area stopping at a table occupied by the most beautiful woman Tron had ever seen. The woman stood up greeting him with her hand outstretch. He took her hand softly placing a kiss on the topside.

"I didn't think there were any more gentlemen left in Houston," she said eloquently batting her eyelashes.

"I didn't think my dreams would ever come true neither," Tron told her, taking a seat after she sat down.

"If you don't mind me asking. How did your dreams all of a sudden become a reality?" she asked, taking a sip of Merlot.

Tron was instantly captivated by her alluring eyes and graceful manners.

"I always dreamed about meeting a woman with such beauty, that made my inner feelings race with excitement," he answered, toying with her proper dialect.

She smiled, displaying a perfect set of white teeth. "I haven't even told you my name yet, and you're laying it on me like a man on a mission," she said, wiping the corners of her mouth with a napkin.

"I'm sorry for getting caught up in your appeal. My name is Tron," he said, reaching his hand across the table for a second contact with her soft velvet hands.

"Nice to meet you Tron, I'm Angelita," she told him. Her heart rate increased a notch at the touch of his hand.

Shaking the naughty thoughts out of her brain, she jumped straight down to business. "Redline spoke very highly of you, so I assume business will be handled accordingly. How many books (KILOS) are you willing to purchase from our company?" Angelita asked, smoothing her dress out over her thighs.

"That all depends on the set price, and the quality of the books,"

Tron replied, surprised by her selection of words and the way she was eying his every move.

"Since Redline referred you to me as a close friend, I feel like I owe him a favor. My prayers go out to him for his recovery. I'll set our price at fifteen-five for fifty books or more,'" Angelita said, raising her hand signaling the waiter.

When Tron heard her mention the word recovery he was puzzled, thinking there was a hidden meaning behind her statement. He stared at the beautiful woman who was hypnotizing him with her scent and finesse. Tron noticed there wasn't a wedding ring on her ring finger. The .10 carat tennis bracelet sparkle on her wrist as she flagged down the waiter.

"Are you two ready to order ma'am?" the waiter asked.

"Yes, I would like the Grandma's Layed salad for an appetizer. And for my main entree, I would like the shrimp fajitas nicely grilled. A bowl of charro beans. Cheese filled enchiladas topped with chili con carna, and beef tacos with rice and refried beans," Angelita said, eyeing the menu.

"Is that all ma'am?" the waiter asked, raising his brows at her.

"I would like a strawberry margarita also please," she said, showcasing her flawless pearl white teeth.

"And you sir!" the waiter asked, focusing on Tron.

"Just give me the pickled gulf shrimp to start with. And let me try the Frito pie with brisket, beans, sausage, chips cheese and the special sauce. And give me a glass of Hennessy on the rocks," Tron said, looking into Angelita's beautiful hazel eyes.

"I'll be back in a minute. Thank you," the waiter said, walking away.

"What do you mean by you hope he recovers?" Tron asked.

"It's been on the news all morning. Redline's girlfriend cut his pene (DICK) off before killing herself." Tron sat there in disbelief, listening to Angelita explain what he had heard on the news earlier. "We hope he pulls through. He's such a major contributor to our family. His business will be highly missed."

Their appetizers arrive and they ate in silence. Angelita's mind was occupied with lustful thoughts of eating Tron for dessert and skipping the main entree. Tron had his own thoughts tumbling over Redline. He knew if Redline didn't survive his chances would be better with Angelita. That would mean more work and clientele. And more money on his behalf. He smiled at the thought of gaining material wealth—the Tony Montana syndrome.

"Do you know what hospital he's in?" he asked.

Angelita didn't hear a word he said sipping her margarita entertain with her own freaky thoughts. "Did you hear me?" Tron asked again, tapping a fork against his glass.

"I'm sorry were you saying something?" Angelita asked, gazing into his eyes.

"I was asking you if you knew what hospital he's in."

"I was told he's in Ben Taub General Hospital. He's on the fourth floor in intensive care," Angelita replied, removing strands of hair away from her face.

They both finished their meal, reaching an agreement on the amount and number of books, along with a drop location. Angelita excused herself to the restroom. Tron quickly stood to his feet helping her slide her chair away from the table. Her scent raped his nostrils, utterly intoxicating. Angelita intentionally brushed up against him. Tron placed his hand on her lower back excusing himself for the contact. Angelita stood in front of him with long black hair flowing down to the middle of her back.

Her complexion was honey brown, with protruding cheekbones. Her body was worthy of an Aztec Princess. Tron gazed at her shapely body sashaying with self-confidence. He felt himself becoming aroused. Angelita had his mind clouded with thoughts of getting between her honey brown thighs. Beautiful women were his weakness, but his love for money placed his brain back on track. Tron gazed as Angelita returning from the restroom. Her presence was magnetic.

The eyes of other customers, male and female looked as she strutted by. Tron stood back to his feet, thinking Salma Hayek would have been jealous of Angelita's beauty.

"Thank you for being a gentleman. I will be in contact with you," she said, shaking his hand before making her exit.

Tron respected her style and the way she walked away without giving him a chance to say anything. He smiled to himself, but the thought of Redline quickly erased it. He knew killing Redline would be a task that needed to be planned to perfection. He sipped the rest of his drink thinking about the last time he was at Ben Taub Hospital...

The day after Redline told him and Lil' Branon about Pee Wee and his homeboy Flagg, Tron took a trip to the hospital. It was easy for him to persuade the receptionist to give him Flagg's location. With a million-dollar smile and topflight conversation, Tron had Flagg's room number in less than two minutes, along with the intern's telephone number. He stood in the room looking down at Flagg thinking back to the day of the shooting. Disguised as a homeless dope fiend, Tron had walked across Belfort street with a spray bottle and a handful of newspapers. He looked into Flagg's eyes as Ralo walked up from behind Pee Wee's car. Tron smiled at Flagg as Ralo's Desert Eagle made its presence known.

Tron snapped out of his daze and noticed a flashing red light on a camera in the top corner of the room. Being attentive paid off for him that day. It saved him a one-way trip to prison for murder. Tron finished his drink leaving a fifty-dollar tip on the table before walking out of the restaurant.

(EVERY OBSTACLE IN LIFE CAN BE HURDLED. SO, IF YOU FAIL BEFORE YOU SUCCEED, DUST YOURSELF OFF AND TRY AGAIN.)

CHAPTER 64

"MIRACULOUS BLESSING"
(BEN TAUB HOSPITAL)
HOUSTON, TEXAS

Redline barely made it to the hospital alive. His pulse was weak. The EMT's expected he was going to die before they arrived. He was rushed straight to the emergency room and prepared for surgery. Redline had to undergo a blood transfusion as soon as he was placed on the operating table. By the grace of GOD his blood type was available.

Hollywood wasn't so lucky. She died because of her love and loyalty. The doctors successfully reattached Redline's penis. He was trans-ferred, to the intensive care unit on the fourth floor. Every personnel in the hospital knew who Adrain Jones was. He was the talk of Hous-ton, Texas, by being in a crime of passion. Redline was oblivious of the visitor walking in. The visitor had a full beard wearing a cowboy hat pull down low on his head. He leaned closely to Redline whispering in his ear.

"Rest in peace pimp!" he said, squeezing off three shots into Redline's face.

The shots from the Glock .24 were silenced by a suppressor. The heart monitor instantly sounded off with a continuous beep. The man quickly exited the room. Sounds of his cowboy boots echoed down the hallway with each step he took. Doctors and nurses ran by him as he made his escape in the opposite direction. Once he made it outside, he slowed down his stride jumping into his vehicle. His heart pumped vigorously slowly driving into traffic.

Scanning his mirrors cautiously, he merged onto the freeway increasing his speed. He snatched off his fake beard and cowboy hat, tossing them on the front seat. His phone vibrated in his pocket.

"Yeah, what's up?" he answered.

"There's a black Escalade parked at your club. Give the money to the driver. Your books are in the white Escalade. The keys are under the left front tire wall. I'll be in touch," Angelita explained, walking into the hospital to visit Redline.

NEVER JUDGE A BOOK BY ITS COVER. NEVER JUDGE A PERSON BY THEIR FIRST IMPRESSION. A BOOK WITH AN UGLY COVER-CAN TURN OUT TO BE VERY GOOD. A PERSON DISPLAYING A GOOD FIRST IMPRESSION...CAN TURN OUT TO BE VERY DECEITFUL.

TO BE CONTINUED...

ALSO BY TERRANCE HOWARD

Trust is the hardest quality to earn, and betrayal is the worse action to overcome. Life consist of both elements, but what will happen when answers are searched for?

Hollywood is a lady looking for answers because she is estranged by the murder of her brother. The only person she trusts is in prison...Redline. While

Hollywood tries to find answers at any cost, she acquires some help in a major way. This poses a problem. The trouble has just got closer like the answer.

Life on the streets of Houston has never been easy, especially with people like Fast Black around. Can Hollywood survive the truth about her brother's death? In due time everything will come to light. So, enter the darkness of the streets ...and let's find out.

OVERBROOK XPRESS PUBLICATIONS PRESENTS

THE Grudge

TERRANCE HOWARD

GRUDGE

A feeling of deep-seated resentment or ill will.

A lot of people hold grudges for many different reasons. Some take their ill feelings down with them to the grave. As for others, they carry out their resentment in a different manner. A very vindictive way to stimulate their sick minded reasons, and personal pleasures.

A grudge...have you ever held one against somebody??? A grudge...what will you do about it??? A grudge...how long will revenge toy with your thoughts??? A grudge..you never know who has one against you!!!

OVERBROOK XPRESS PUBLICATIONS PRESENTS

Dangerous
DESIRES

TERRANCE
HOWARD

Coty Cole, a young undercover federal agent with a point to prove. She was chosen by her superior commander to go undercover as a prison guard in a all male prison to obtain incriminating evidence on an infamous drug lord from Houston, Texas.

Larry Smith, aka Bull, ran a tight organization on the Northside of Houston. Even behind concrete walls and steel bars, he continued to control the streets quite impressively, as well as the drug flow in prison.

Will Coty Cole be able to stay focused and control her lustful hormones??? Or will the curiosity of her kitty Kat lead her to DANGEROUS DESIRES

CONNECT WITH TERRANCE

overbrookxpresspublications@gmail.com

instagram.com/overbrook_xpress_publications

COVER & LAYOUT DESIGN
BY

A company designed with Urban Lit in mind, NubianFX combines innovative visuals dipped in melanin swag. Get Book covers, graphics, photography & more!

NUBIANFX CREATE COVERS & DESIGN